Glimmerglass

MERCER
UNIVERSITY PRESS

Endowed by
TOM WATSON BROWN
and
THE WATSON-BROWN FOUNDATION, INC.

GLIMMERGLASS

A NOVEL

MARLY YOUMANS

MERCER UNIVERSITY PRESS
MACON, GEORGIA
35 Years of Publishing Excellence

MUP/ H896

Published by
Mercer University Press
Macon, Georgia 31207

© 2014 Marly Youmans

Cover and interior art by Clive Hicks-Jenkins.

9 8 7 6 5 4 3 2 1

Books published by Mercer University Press
are printed on acid-free paper that meets the
requirements of the American National Standard
for Information Sciences—Permanence of Paper
for Printed Library Materials.

Library of Congress Cataloging-in-Publication Data

Youmans, Marly.
  Glimmerglass : a novel / Marly Youmans.
    pages cm
  ISBN 978-0-88146-491-7 (hardback : acid-free paper)
  ISBN 0-88146-491-0 (hardback : acid-free paper)
   I. Title.
   PS3575.O68G57 2014
  813'.54—dc23

2014015616

Books by Marly Youmans

NOVELS

A Death at the White Camellia Orphanage

Val/Orson

The Wolf Pit

Catherwood

Little Jordan

POETRY

Thaliad

The Foliate Head

The Throne of Psyche

Claire

SOUTHERN FANTASIES

Ingledove

The Curse of the Raven Mocker

for Yolanda Sharpe and Ashley Norwood Cooper

—artists near Glimmerglass & Kingfisher—

CONTENTS

The blossoms fallen, the sap gone from the tree,
The broken monuments of my great desires…

Out of that mass of miracles, my muse
Gathered those flowers to her pure senses pleasing…

—Sir Walter Ralegh,
The Ocean to Cynthia, c. 1589

The Gatehouse

Cottage of the Dwarves

She waited at the edge of the lane for half an hour, long enough for any surprise over the griffins and the iron curlicues above the entrance to have melted away. Glints of lake showed through a screen of trees, some bare, some evergreen.

When the neighbor showed up, Cynthia felt a flick of curiosity. This wizened creature, face finely pleated and hair in a tangle, looked as though all its bones had been broken and then carelessly reset.

"Isabelle Hix—H-i-x—call me Iz—did they say?"

So the figure was not *it* but *she*...

Cynthia shook her head, bemused by the dry, cricket-like voice, so in keeping with the body. *Iz Hix.*

"They wouldn't, would they? Much too grand for that. Let Iz take care of things. Iz can do it." The key was dark on her palm. "You didn't need this—half the doors have nothing but a latch."

"Oh, I could've gone inside without bothering you. I'm sorry. I don't really know anything. A girl at Moon Gate gave me directions and told me when to show up." Cynthia decided that Iz must have been hurt in an accident—she could see pale needle-lines of scars on her hands and a slash along one cheekbone.

"That's all right. It's a bit lonesome here. Good to know you have a neighbor. And if you have trouble with *them*, you can tell me. They're cousins of mine. Somewhat removed, if you take my meaning."

Cynthia wondered whether Iz thought that she had agreed to rent. Yet she hadn't even made up her mind to move anywhere, much less to the village of Cooper Patent, an assemblage of shops and houses on the southern tip of Glimmerglass. By chance she had lit on the lake and village and wandered into Moon Gate, where she overheard the clerk talking about the cottage. The tiny seed of an idea had come to her—now to be planted or not.

"I haven't seen the place before, and don't know if I'll want it."

Iz nodded. "I expect you will. Plenty of people around here would give their eyeteeth to live in the gatehouse—lots

4

of charm, perfectly cunning, wildlife all around. But it's not the most comfortable place in the world."

She pointed to some flagstones between firs. "That's the path."

Cynthia followed the other woman, reaching up a hand to protect her face from the switch of branches. Beyond the trees, the cottage was low and small with a portico of arches and leaded glass in the heavy door.

"We'll go in the right way." Iz worked the key back and forth in the lock until the teeth caught and the bolt made a snapping noise. "Here. You take it. Rent due at month's end. No deposit. They're easygoing, maybe too much so."

Although Cynthia started to say again that she hadn't committed to the house, she accepted the key, noticing that the outstretched hand smelled strongly of smoke. Crossing the threshold, she found herself in a parlor with a carved stone fireplace and more leaded glass windows. Her eye was drawn to the low ceiling, sprinkled with flora and fauna in low white relief—a thistle and a pomegranate, a flaming salamander, an English lion, a goose, a weasel, and a dragon biting its own tail.

"Like clouds," she exclaimed, at once feeling pleased.

"Very like." Iz glanced into the garden. "Nothing much left. The scilla and snowdrops are sending up sprouts all over again, just in time for a frost kill. Stupid things."

Cynthia slipped into the next chamber, finding another row of leaded panes and a passage to the outside. Peeping through a window slot in the door, she saw further exits leading onto a grassy courtyard and flowerbeds. The house was in the shape of the letter U, with the open end bounded by a ribbon of grass next to a creek of boulders and moss and overhanging limbs.

"It's the cottage of the seven dwarves." She spoke to no one at all, but Iz heard her from the next room and rasped out that she would have to be Snow White.

"Funny sort of Snow White," Cynthia whispered. Perhaps not as odd as Iz would be, but she was far beyond such roles....

And there hadn't been a prince. Or there had, and she had married him and found that he was manic mad, a card-carrying member of the Hatter tribe, with a joker and a bottle in his pocket. Their bungalow had reeked of dope and been loud with howls against boss and job. He had danced like the Witch in red-hot slippers, stamping in frenzy, and at last jigged off with another woman. To torment her in turn, Cynthia supposed.

She felt a twinge of something mixed and unclear— remorse blended with relief and sadness—remembering how he would jerk his head to look at her, his profile elegant against the light. She made a noise of disgust. To think so, after all these years!

"What do you do? Are you taking a job in the village? You're not local, or I'd know." Iz's voice grated its way into her thoughts.

"I'm—"

She had almost said that she was an artist, but it wasn't true. It hadn't been so for a long time. "I do watercolors of houses, or copies of family photographs. I sell a lot of prints of street scenes in tourist towns like Newport and Saratoga."

Iz made a noncommittal sound.

"What—"

Again Cynthia paused. Perhaps Iz couldn't work, given her crooked bones and scars that signaled some past disaster.

"I'm just a gimp." Iz passed by, wielding a broom, and winked at her. "Can't stand cobwebs," she said, shaking the handle.

She had spoken cheerfully. All the same, there seemed to be no proper response.

Perhaps I'm a kind of gimp, too, Cynthia reflected. In the last year she had felt nipped by darkness. Small diabolic forces seemed arrayed against her, peppering her with ill thoughts.

She leaned her forehead against the leaded glass and looked out at the hollyhocks—their seeds buttoned up for winter, with only a few flowers like pink crepe paper left on the stalks—and at Michaelmas daisies and misguided spring bulbs with shoots pushing up crumbs of earth. She was glad to see their bravery, and there was something consoling about the perfect shapes, motionless in the cold air.

"There are seven doors to the outside," Iz announced, dragging the broom as she wandered by.

"Of course there are," Cynthia murmured.

"Tatty old webs." When Iz waved the broom, a streamer of cobwebbing wafted up from the lintel.

"What about bugs? I don't much care for insects."

7

"Sure, there are a few—earwigs, mostly, or a millipede now and then. Doodlebugs go trundling about the doorstep. But the salamanders in the cellar eat them."

"Salamanders in the cellar?"

"Cute little things," Iz said. "They won't come upstairs. It's too dry."

Cynthia felt the oddity of it all. Imagine: salamanders lived below the floorboards, holding still, or darting like a flame in the dark. Would there be a lion roaring in the wood, a weasel at the brook, and thistles in the garden? She would expect pomegranates at the village grocery.

Iz shouldered her weapon, marching toward the kitchen. In a minute, she stuck her head back through the doorway. "Go on around the other arm of the house; there's a pretty good bath and a couple of bedrooms."

Glad to explore without a chaperone, Cynthia nodded obediently, her fingers brushing up against the cool plaster walls of the dining room. Next came the parlor with its clouds and after that a long whitewashed hall running alongside a bedroom and bath. The floors were uneven, the clumsy sills cut from logs. At a quirk in the passage, she peered into a north-lit room that could be a studio. Last of all was a larger chamber illumined by early autumn sunshine, the shafts slanting through the deep-set windows.

Yes, this could be her bedroom, with pictures, antiques, and a spool bed with jacquard coverlet. The austere light struck at her, made her feel like a solitary anchored in a cell. The effect was grief, and it made her think, as she had so often lately, that she had made too many wrong choices. Now she would never bear the children she had imagined, never sit in a sunny window while her daughter glued sequins onto the glittering hoard under a paper dragon's thigh, never be asked unexpected questions about death and sex and the invisibles of the world, and never kneel to rock a boy in her arms— comforting him for his older brother or sister's slight, feeling the crown of his head warm against her cheek.

On a window ledge Cynthia saw a book, splayed open, and picked it up. The title did not interest her, but she skimmed a starred passage marked *childhood* in the margin: "The green trees when I saw them first through one of the gates transported and ravished me, their sweetness and unusual beauty made my heart to leap, and almost mad with ecstasy, they were such strange and wonderful things… Boys and girls tumbling in the street, and playing, were moving jewels."

All day, magical gates, she thought. And here were children again, as if in answer to her feeling of loss.

A fresh fear gave her a pang: that she had given over all chance of looking with infant sight at a world made new. And what was that but the beginning of art? Reflected in the panes, her eyes seemed sad, infiltrated by shadows.

Iz was leaning in the door. "Check the flyleaf," she said, and Cynthia thumbed to the front of the book.

"Lydia Lanier, New Orleans."

"Oh, that's our rector's wife, Lydia Wren. She's a piece of work. I like her, mind you. She's full of original vim."

"Maybe you'd like to give the book back."

9

"No, you take it to her. Then you'll know two people." Iz peered out the window. "Think I'll sweep the flagstones. Looks like the stream left a bunch of trash."

"I haven't agreed to move," Cynthia said, but Iz was already gone. "I really haven't," she told the empty room. "And I don't know where Lydia Wren lives, or anything."

Venturing into the courtyard, she found that Iz was still talking about the book's owner. "You can't miss her," she was saying. "Rectory right next to the church, near the river, a block off the main street. Funny lady. Writes a column for the newspaper. Lydia, I mean."

"Maybe," Cynthia began.

"Besides, there's Father Hale, too. Hale Wren. Wonderful man."

Cynthia glanced at the trellises with their dried relics of clematis and at the spray ricocheting off the stones in the ravine. She remembered her mother's voice, impatient and worried: *Do some painting, go to church, and get a life, Cyn.* But she had ignored the advice. It had taken her years to get over Colm.

"A few people won't have any part of the place," Iz called. "Did they tell you? My precious cousins? 'Course not. A few years ago the beavers abandoned this piece of the creek and started to build higher, and afterward their old dam broke and the water ripped through the gulch and flooded the house. The stove and fridge ended up flip-flopped on the far side of the kitchen. The watermark inside was four feet. They've had it all painted since."

Cynthia stepped back, eyeing the watercourse.

"Could happen again," Iz said, her voice as bright as a gong that trembles with warning. "Lucky thing nobody was in the gatehouse. I knew a fellow who was fishing at the edge of Glimmerglass. He heard a sound like thunder and spied a jumble of trees riding on the flood, slamming straight toward him. He started running for his life."

"Did he catch it?" Cynthia pictured the man chasing a white wisp through the shallows.

"He got himself safe home," Iz said.

In a blink of fright, Cynthia saw the churning stream dash itself against the flimsily latched doors—she tripped, and the waters plunged her to the matting and shoved murk into her mouth.

It doesn't matter. Hadn't she often thought of life as a surreal landscape pitted with trap doors that could collapse at one wrong footstep? Yes, she would move here and rent the gatehouse. Like a tropical stalk erupting in a New England garden plot, whim shot up and flowered. She would be proud and careless and not afraid of an animal hovel of sticks, hurled pell-mell to the shore.

Her reflected face, crosshatched by the lead seams of a window, gleamed pale and transparent.

"Are there ghosts?"

But Iz didn't hear over the frolics of the water, and she had to ask again.

"Ghosts? Nothing but what you bring, I expect," Iz said, not pausing in her sweeping.

Cynthia's glance settled on the trees across the stream.

Who didn't have ghosts? And she was diminishing, changing—her face momentarily strange in the glass. She had hold of the tail end of middle age; she was an attractive woman, often mistaken for one much younger. Her hair still shone black, with only sparse threads of snow, and her skin was unwrinkled. There might be something left for her, here in the gatehouse beyond the village. Hadn't she long ago combed her hair with the teeth of pain, eaten the poisoned apple, and married the prince of fire? What more could hurt her now? Perhaps she would at last sketch and paint just for herself. Something not yet glimpsed would console her for the princes who would not do, and the children she might have borne, and the high art that had failed her: the art that she had failed.

In October the cold would seal the stream in ice. Snow would sag the limbs outside the kitchen window and turn the world stainless, as if it knew nothing of blood and dirty deeds. She would build a snow maiden in the courtyard and feed the birds that had the courage to stay and not fly south. Perhaps she could seek and find new comforters—those little bearded men with the merry eyes, eternally glad that she had not stayed in the tower with the prince but had at last returned home. On sunny days she would open wide the seven doors to let them come in.

A Cup of Music, a Hill of Sea

The hat was a monstrous, flaring creation, stuck round with faux birds, out-of-date opera tickets, a skull made out of sugar, a miniature Red Sox pennant, a pin in the shape of a musical note, and a bunch of silk wisteria.

"Oh!" Lydia tweaked the brim. "It's my alms-for-the-poor-and-benighted hat. Every day until the last, somebody makes a pledge and gets to fasten a memento to the hat. It gets awfully heavy sometimes. Once a friend tried to add a stuffed peacock with the feathers fanned out. After that I said, 'No taxidermy. And none of your fancy blue chickens!'

It was just the third day, too, and he wanted the corpse returned in good shape. No pledge is big enough to carry a ten-pound bird on my head for weeks."

"Wouldn't be for me. I've never heard of such a thing," Cynthia said.

"I invented it." Lydia gave a little flourish of the hand. "Begging is a dreadfully boring thing. This is easier and more amusing, and nobody ever forgets when a drive is on. I do a hat once a year, or as the spirit takes me."

"It's the quirkiest way of—"

"We have to be a tad over the top in this town." Lydia untied the hat, set it on a table, and picked up the volume Cynthia had found in the empty gatehouse and was now, a month later, at last returning. "Thank you for rescuing my book. I just love Traherne, don't you? And wondered where he had rambled off to... I must have loaned it to Jenny Wild, when she was staying there. What was I saying before? Oh, *over the top*. This is the most eccentric place I've ever lived. That's saying a lot because I grew up in a peculiar corner of Louisiana. Perhaps this is only equal to it, but then there's the whole Yankee thing. Yankees are not a bit like Louisianans, and they're odd, very odd." She fluffed her curls where they had been squashed by the hat. "I don't suppose I'll ever get over the way Yankees are," she reflected, "even though I married one."

Cynthia did not know what to reply to this. Being a Northerner herself, she was not sure whether to feel vaguely insulted. But Lydia did not let the silence lie fallow for long.

14

"You're a painter, Iz Hix tells me. I'd like to come see your pictures," she announced. "Teddy Wild's going to ask you to paint a portrait of Andrew and one of himself for Sea House. You haven't met them yet, but you will. They're interesting. Colorful."

"What? I've never even heard of them." Cynthia was startled. Then, after a moment or two, she found that she was pleased.

As a young woman, she had been told that her talent lay in portraiture and that she possessed a rare facility with the human figure. This surprisingly old-fashioned verdict of her instructors had led her to focus on oils. But it hadn't been easy to combine painting with married life, and so she found a niche in tourism, sketching and painting historic sites. She thought it a lucky chance at the time, though later she wondered whether the first commission had been a kind of devil's bargain, to make sure that she would fail at what she had meant to do.

Lydia had gone on talking, though Cynthia hadn't heard any of it and now caught only the last of her words: "as they have a picture of every ancestor and most family members, except a cousin who died young, and Teddy thought that he might ask you."

"I haven't met a Wild—"

"You mean you don't know the Wild brothers? Isn't that funny…didn't anybody tell you?"

Cynthia looked from Lydia to the hat. The rector's wife loved mysteries, it seemed. She wondered if the whole village would prove as novel as Lydia Wren and Iz Hix.

"No matter," Lydia said airily, "it will be more fun to find out for yourself."

But it wasn't until some weeks later that Cynthia realized her link to the brothers.

———

Plink.

Plink-a-plinkplink.

Thunkplink.

Earlier, the fierce popping from a green branch had kept her from falling asleep on the rug. Now and then came a *hissss* and much spitting as a fat September raindrop sank down the chimney and was transformed by flames. So when the first tear splashed her on the neck, Cynthia thought of the fire. Another struck her cheek. She looked at the ceiling and saw water pooling on a plaster swan's wing. She held up her teacup—a chipped flow blue sprinkled with shamrocks—and caught a plummeting drop.

When one splattered on the chest that served as a tea table, she scrambled to her feet. Soon a bowl in the rich green glaze called *Chinese blue* and a pot from the kitchen were making music with the teacup, the pot sounding hollow and reverberant next to the *ting! ting! ting!* and *plink-a-tink* of the other two.

She couldn't get Iz Hix on the phone. She wasn't surprised, as Iz seemed the sort of person who would choose not to obey a ring and not to be at the beck of an answering machine.

16

After tossing the collected drops onto the fire and watching as late afternoon sun dispersed the storm clouds, she decided that a trip to Iz's house might be better than a call.

Outside, rain that had pooled in the hollows of the steps soaked her low-sided shoes. Cold felt good on her face as she pulled out of the driveway and onto the lake road.

She knew the turnoff to the house but hadn't realized that the drive was only one lane. Raspberry bushes hung over the blacktop, dripping diamonds, and the canes made screaky noises against the enameled hood. When the car broke through the shrubbery, she stared: one side of the sky was bright, with a rainbow and its echo standing among the trees, while the other was indigo—a cloud moving slowly away.

Hardly noticing how she parked, Cynthia got out and stood staring. She thought of the pad and watercolor pencils stowed in the trunk but rejected the idea. Sketches with rainbows were almost always sentimental. Yet she couldn't stop looking. Not until a wisp of the second rainbow had entirely vanished and the first had come close to being invisible did she step toward the house.

She would never have imagined that Iz owned such an impressive Georgian pile, with a big Palladian window on the second story. The masonry was a marvel, so varied in its components and yet so tight, but its harmony seemed at odds with how the wings—she guessed them to be later additions—crumbled into the exposed rocks and soil of the hillside. Perhaps the rear of the central portion was the same. Noticing an abundance of fossils in the walls, she paused to search and spotted a small, bony fish and what appeared to be the thorax of a trilobite.

The bronze doorknocker had been cast in the form of a lithe water dragon, a serpentine tail neatly grasped in its jaws. It stared at her with eyes of inlaid bloodstone.

Her fingers moved lightly over the scales, and at last she seized the creature about the body and rapped firmly. Reflecting that Iz might not be so easy to summon, she decided to wait ten minutes for a response. Her glance wandered from a topiary yew cut into the shape of a bowler hat to a flagstone walk winding between trees to a blue clearing in the sky.

But she did not have to idle long.

"Yes?" The door swung open, and in the dark hallway stood a little figure in a bottle-green suit and canary vest.

Cynthia's eyes rose from the splash of yellow to the face, boyish but not a boy's. A nebula of silky hair gleamed above the dome of his head, and his cheeks were red and round: in all, giving the impression of an ancient juvenile.

"I was looking for"—and here she ran through the list of "Ms. Hix, Isabelle Hix, Iz Hix" before settling on the last.

"Isabelle doesn't live here!" The man laughed merrily and cried out, "We couldn't possibly have Izzie Hix here, could we, Andrew?"

"No—mercy, mercy, what a thought." The voice drifted to them from a distance, and in a few moments its owner followed.

"I'm from the gatehouse," Cynthia was saying. "Sorrel. I'm Cynthia Sorrel. And I just wanted to let Iz know that the parlor is leaking. She told me to call if there were any problems. I'd hate for the wonderful motifs on the ceiling to be lost—"

"Well, he's my brother Andrew"—the man in the yellow vest gestured behind him—"and I'm Theodore. Theodore and Andrew Wild." He said the words with no little satisfaction.

They don't look a bit alike, Cynthia thought.

"We're half-brothers, you know," he added softly, as if reading her mind. "And the best of friends. Incorrigible bachelors, the pair of us."

She shook hands, wondering if Theodore added the last as a warning whenever a woman came to the door. It had the ring of something often said.

"Welcome to the village—welcome to Sea House." Andrew's hand was a strong grasp, in contrast with the slack, plump hand of his brother.

Younger, Cynthia decided, *Andrew must be the younger.* He had the kind of face often called *craggy*—jutting cheekbones, strong jaw—and a mass of thick hair. *Prematurely white,* she judged. As they chatted, she took notice of the laugh lines around his blue eyes, the readiness to be pleased, and the worn tweed jacket and thought that he must be a comfortable sort of person to have around. It would be Theodore who annoyed, wouldn't it? *Prim,* she thought, *a touch of prissiness about him.*

She had asked about the name of the place, and now Andrew was explaining that it was because of the fossils— the mason having been a bit of a hobbyist—set around the door and strewn over the front.

"In the nineteenth century, visitors often claimed that they could hear the roar of a withdrawing tide during the night and sometimes a whistling or a rhythmic thudding. It must've been the wind or footsteps reverberating in the hallways. A more fanciful age, I expect. Though my brother and I sometimes have wild thoughts, living here, don't we, Teddy? It's the way the house goes back into the hill. A bit eerie."

"Wild thoughts indeed." Theodore winked. "What other kind could we have, being *Wild* ourselves? Won't you walk in, Mrs. Sorrel?"

"Call me Cynthia, please—and I'm not married."

"Please stay, at least for a moment," Andrew said. "You're almost our nearest neighbor, so we've been remiss in not coming by to see you."

Though she hadn't meant to venture inside, she let the brothers usher her into a small parlor. Evidently the two had been drinking tea when she interrupted them, and next to the pot were Tenby tarts and shortbread dipped in chocolate and other pastries she couldn't quite identify, all made "by our own Mr. Llewellyn. He comes to the farmer's market every Saturday, and I hie there with a basket and buy him out, I'm afraid."

Theodore's voice squeaked as he made this admission, and Cynthia smothered a laugh—the friendly little animals of *The Wind in the Willows* with their waterside picnic and their hearthside toast had popped into her head.

But Andrew was more attractive to her, with a warmth that made her feel glad she had come, as if she had been invited especially.

The brothers were pleasant hosts. As if by sleight of hand, she instantly acquired a translucent cup so pretty that she felt like peeking beneath to find out the maker, along with a plate serving an old-fashioned thing that Theodore said was a Maid of Honor.

"Oh, I get it—like a Renaissance girl, all powdered and fat-bellied." She regarded the cake with pleasure. It had magically called up a long-ago history class and a soon-to-be-pregnant, ceruse-painted Maid of Honor, her skirts hauled to the waist in the Queen's garden. The girl had called out *Sweet Sir Walter! Sweet Sir Walter!* until the words slurred into *swisher swasher! swisher swasher!* Afterward, hadn't Elizabeth immured Ralegh in the Tower of London for getting Bess Throckmorten with child?

"How funny," she said, "and delicious."

"Have another," Theodore offered.

"Have three." Andrew passed the tray of sweets.

"I couldn't," she said, but took a piece of shortbread.

"I could. In fact, I will," said Theodore, "because I am completely without self-control."

Oh, she liked the half-brothers and the parlor with yellow drapes and Sea House, peppered with fossils. The enchantment of past times lapped over her. Perhaps fossils from an absent ocean were the reason they fell to reminiscing about childhood trips to Cape Cod and Martha's Vineyard. She wasn't surprised to find that the suntanned Andrew loved to sail.

After tea, the elder Wild guided her through the downstairs rooms, though she could hardly take in the profusion of architectural ornament, family furniture, and paintings crackled by age. "Flotsam and jetsam," Andrew called it. He trailed behind them, cup in hand, occasionally making a comment.

At one door they stopped, and Theodore put his ear against it.

"There! The song of the sea. You try."

Cynthia obeyed and heard a faint, shell-like sonority.

"It's the dark, breathing. We never go there anymore." Andrew slid a hand over the paneled door. "When we were boys, my cousins and I went into the hill many times, always with an uncle. Teddy used to go with us when he was visiting. My thirteenth birthday was the first and last time we went alone."

"One of them never came back." Theodore looked at her, eyes shining.

"What do you mean?" Cynthia withdrew her hand from the doorknob. For one weird instant, she had felt that the pulsing sound was falling into the syllables of her name.

"Did you see, as we moved toward the hill, how the rooms dwindle, and the halls aren't spacious and straight but shrink and waver? The house starts turning into something else." The little man looked at her with glee, and Cynthia remembered the innocent, sexless dwarfs who loved Snow White, and the seven doors to the gatehouse, one for each dwarf. *He ought to live there*, she thought, *with the salamanders*.

"Theodore—"

"Just call him *Teddy*," Andrew told her. "Nobody really calls him *Theodore*, or even *Theo*, unless they're mad at him. It was never a fit."

22

Theodore—now transformed to *Teddy*—frowned, but Andrew didn't notice. Instead, he moved away from the door, his gaze unfocused.

"The one who didn't return was my favorite cousin," he said. "It's dank in there, and sometimes I can't help thinking that the house is a grave."

"That's cheerful," Teddy said.

Andrew gave a shake of the head, as if to scatter dark thoughts. "How we've been gossiping! Cynthia must think us quite strange."

"No, I…"

I like it here, she thought. *It's not anything I would have imagined.*

Teddy stopped to hold a door for her, and she left the shadow of the hill behind. Spindly light from the windows made her recall the outer world and what she had come for, but it didn't matter now. She was charmed by the brothers, and the house of tattered splendor and stone sea creatures had cast a spell on her.

"With all the fossils, this might as well be the oldest house in the world. And yesterday, when I met Lydia Wren, she told me that Cooper Patent is the most eccentric village in all fifty states. So I suppose you have a duty to be strange," she said, "if you are."

Andrew laughed, though he had been somber only a moment before. "Hear that, Teddy? We have a license to be odd."

"Such a relief," his half-brother cried, throwing open a pair of double doors onto another of the endless prospects of china and glass and drape and Persian carpet, as lavish and dreamlike as bandit treasure pillaged from the *Arabian Nights.*

She stepped across a bright threshold and another and another, feeling unexpectedly happy and only pausing once—to meet the eyes of a painted lady wearing an arabesque swoop of a hat. *Lydia's hat,* Cynthia remembered, conjuring their meeting in one glad flash of memory.

"Shall we have the gatehouse repaired for you and not bother Iz?" Andrew's voice startled her.

"Oh, no, thank you—"

"That's the sort of thing you pay Iz for, Andrew," Teddy said. "She gets the gardener's house and an allowance, you see," he explained, "and we give Cousin Isabelle errands to make her feel useful. Be useful, if she can."

"So." The note of surprise sounded bell-like in the passage. "That's what Lydia meant! You two must be my landlords—"

"Not I," Teddy said, dusting his hands together.

"Don't think of it that way! We need someone in the gatehouse, or else the place would be a moldy old horror inside six months. It's a privilege to have you there," Andrew said, swinging open the front door. Cold pressed into the entrance hall.

Teddy gestured at the lane. "If you want to tell Izzie yourself, she's only a few hundred yards up the lane."

As Cynthia passed from hall to porch, she was still adjusting her mind to the idea that the gatehouse belonged to the mansion.

"A long time ago," she said slowly, "I suppose the gatehouse wasn't divided from this one by the lake road, and anybody coming here would have to go through the arch."

"That's right. It's too bad," Teddy said. "Changes tend to be so ugly."

"They're not in the same style, are they? I'm sorry that I didn't realize who—"

"Don't think anything of it," Andrew said. "We don't. Once I lived in the gatehouse with my wife. I always like to see the creek and cottage and a glimpse of lake through the trees. It reminds me of youth—we married in our teens. Our children are living in town, and they don't care so much for the Wild estate, though I imagine the eldest will live here when Teddy and I are gone."

He glanced up at the sky, now a watercolor wash in shades of blue and gray.

"I'll see her to the car," Teddy announced, patting his half-brother's shoulder. "I wanted to talk about painting and never quite did, did I?" He held out an arm to Cynthia, and she accepted it, touched by his old-fashioned courtesy. "We'll have that chat next time," he promised.

The air nudged against them, cool and heavy, as they navigated the front walk.

"Andrew took our cousin's death hard," he said, lowering his voice, "and only two years later he managed to get a girl pregnant. It was quite the village tempest. The poor things had a fiery go of it, being married and parents so young."

When they looked back at the house, Andrew had gathered his thoughts and was following.

"Marian—the child bride—she died, you know," Teddy whispered. "Lupus. It made her difficult. She wouldn't take care of herself and do what the doctors said. Stubborn girl. She lost her foot at forty and then her leg to the knee—"

"I'm so—"

"Come back to see us." Andrew had caught up with them and now enclosed her hand in his. "Too much alone, aren't we, Teddy? Being shut up with dour painted faces of ancestors and echoes from the hill probably makes us unfit for company."

"No, not at all. Thank you for asking me in. I enjoyed my tea and tour very much." Cynthia marveled at the pair, Theodore-called-Teddy like a Tweedledee and Andrew like a retired sea captain, washed up on a fossil ocean. She would remember them for a long time, one bent, listening at the door into the hill, the other with his hands out, explaining—the yellow vest and Andrew's hair making splotches of brightness in the gloom.

I'd like to paint them.

"Yes, I would," she said aloud. She thought it no wonder that they didn't bother to trim the overgrown lane—why shouldn't the road and the land overlap, when house was hill and hill was house?

Iz in Smoke

At the gardener's cottage, she rapped with a knocker in the shape of a spade; it reminded her more of graves than gardens, as did the porch's flowerless urns, packed with earth. Lying on its back next to one of the jars was a bronze minotaur in acute need of a scrub and some polishing, his bull's eyes bulging as he took in Cynthia and the sky. Engraved letters under his feet read *Somnium*.

"Hello there, Somnium," she said, and knocked again.

The untended aspect of the place suggested a for-gotten mausoleum. She lingered on the steps, wondering if Iz would answer the door.

"Heaving up the lid on the coffin takes time," Cynthia murmured, hearing a distant slam. The minotaur continued to stare. A sound as of slippers scuffing against the floor, a tinkering with latches and chains... the door cracked open. For some moments there was no other sign of any welcome. Then the door drifted inward until the narrow figure of Iz was exposed.

"Sorry." The eyes under the thicket of hair blinked at the sun. "I'm not being very hospitable. Come in."

"That's all right. I just wanted to say that there's a leak in the parlor ceiling." She slipped inside and followed Iz down the hall. In a living room spare almost to emptiness, a wall of French doors overlooked a stretch of lawn and a bedraggled cottage garden.

Cynthia breathed shallowly, and her nose felt pinched. Skeins of tobacco smoke drifted near the ceiling, and the whole atmosphere of the place held quiet and still, as if half smothered.

"Teddy said that I should tell you." She wondered whether it would be rude to leave immediately.

"Yes, that's how it goes. Iz this, Iz that—"

"I could call—"

"No, no. Can't have you phoning up carpenters. It's my job, you see. To take care of things for them. The Hix fix. They're not very good at looking after themselves, so I have to do it." Iz lifted a smeared glass and drained the contents, but she didn't offer anything to her neighbor.

28

"Well," Cynthia began.

"Deep subject." Iz's laugh seemed scraped from a throat of bone. "Sorry. That's the world's oldest joke, isn't it? Listen, I'll have the roof checked. I'll have Jack Gimble stop by before the week's out, or his son, or somebody."

"Thank you. I'm afraid I can't stay." Cynthia was having some difficulty linking this Iz with the one who had brought the key to the gatehouse. The free, acerbic spirit seemed more abrasive than it had earlier. Fine white splinters gleamed on her face. "I'm heading out for supplies, but I was worried about that pretty ceiling."

Iz came close, tapped hard on Cynthia's breastbone.

"You want to watch out for my cousins. Theodore, he's coconut salad. As for Andrew—"

Cynthia was startled to find that she felt offended on behalf of the brothers.

"I found your cousins charming. I must go, Iz. And I hope you'll take care of the roof." The brisk tone sounded alien to her ears. Wainscoting clung to her sweater, and she jerked her arm away, the wall feeling unpleasantly tacky to her fingertips.

"He got my inheritance, you know. Great-grandmother Alice always said I was her pet. Andrew let Teddy live with him at Sea House after Marian died, but I had to be shunted off to the gardener's shed."

She sounds about twelve, Cynthia thought, surprised all over again by feeling sorry for Iz.

"It's a lovely cottage," she said. "And I'd be pleased to live here. Just as pleased as I am to be in the gatehouse."

29

"You know what the children used to say? Izzie Hix, ugly sticks. They still look at me that way in the village shops." The woman's sharp, unexpected laugh pierced the cloudy air.

Cynthia edged toward the door, one hand raised to ward off the smoke. "Perhaps you should go lie down."

From the threshold, Iz looked like an imp, her face crumpled, one leg drawn up a little ways as though she were about to hop in gleeful triumph. Smoke seemed to have gathered around her like a cocoon.

"Good-bye," Cynthia said, her hand clutching at the knob. She did not wait for any reply from Iz. A wall of smoke pressed against her as if it meant to keep her in the house, but she tore through the fragile barrier and into the light.

On shutting the door, she felt as pleased with the intense green lawn studded with red and yellow maple leaves and the salmon-colored chrysanthemums and the blue asters as if she had found the gate to Eden. She bent to brush a cobweb from her legs and noticed that the bronze head of the minotaur seemed to wear a faint, welcoming smile. For a moment, she fancied that the half-human creature could know what she was feeling and sympathize.

So long, Somnium...

She straightened and took in great lungfuls of air, gasping at the cold. It tasted faintly of pears.

"Thought I liked her that day, though she wasn't particularly nice," Cynthia whispered. "She was interesting. But I don't care for her after all, poor thing."

The Boy in the Trees

You're not listening to me one whit!" Lydia was laughing at her.

"No," Cynthia confessed, "Because I was remembering what you said before—about the oddness of the town."

"And you haven't even met Hale yet. He's a snort of the real Old Peculier. You'll have to come to church on Sunday."

"All right, maybe I will. I haven't been in years. I suppose that's wicked of me," she said.

"Of course it's wicked of you," Lydia said gaily, tying on her hat. It had acquired new decorations, including a plastic fish, a tiny blue chicken, and a doll's high-heel shoe, scaled in red sequins.

By Sunday, Cynthia forgot about church entirely and was out early, huddled in a jacket. The wind tossed handfuls of steam from her cup. On the other side of the creek, fog had settled in a vivid mass of plants she could not identify, some red-leaved and thorny, some yellow, some evergreen.

So the whiteness that glimmered in the branches didn't catch her notice as anything more than a glimpse of pallor in the motley scene. She must have been looking straight at him for several moments, her hands warmed by the mug and her thoughts absent, before she took in more than leaves.

A boy was standing in the gangly maples behind the thicket. He was looking in the direction of Sea House and the unkempt area beyond, where the beavers built their dams and the deer clustered in winter, safe on posted land. She guessed that he might be seventeen or thereabouts. He wasn't equipped for a ramble—in fact, he was shirtless, though his skin showed no trace of tan.

Slowly the boy turned his head until he stared directly at her.

What was left of the artist in her felt the glance like a hard slap. He was simply not like anything she had seen before, his face appearing beautiful though irregular, eyes a startling blue even from a distance, and skin shining as the droplets of mist around him caught the sun. Cynthia forgot all else, drinking in the sight like a woman who has been thirsty for years. It was not about physical desire, though he had manifested as simply as the god Eros and shot a bolt at her heart. Her hand trembled as he vanished in a rustle of boughs. She saw a gleam of white, and at once it was gone.

She breathed out a long-held snatch of air. When she spoke, her voice was only a whisper.

"What a queer place I've come to!" Queer, she thought, in an ancient, nigh-magical sense, crooked and foreign, stirring with beings alien to the daily world of getting and selling.

"I'd like to sketch him," she added, and pondered what it would entail.

Then, finally remembering her casual assent to Lydia, she impulsively decided to visit the church.

After trading jeans for a skirt, Cynthia drove into the village and pulled into a spot near the lych gate. "Already started," she murmured, "it must be." She hurried up the aisle of crabapple trees leading to the door. Despite the windows closed for fall, she could hear an organ with trumpet pipes.

Such a pretty Gothic church, she noted, passing from sun to shadow to the lights of the sanctuary.

Lydia was in the choir, hat bobbing as she sang. A festoon of electric blue dangled from the brim of the fundraiser, which contrasted oddly with her choir robes.

It must be getting rather heavy, Cynthia thought, glancing about at stained-glass windows and marble tablets on the rose-adobe walls. But before the song finished up with a joyous hurdy-gurdy flourish from the organ, the choir and priest marched out, leaving the acolytes to douse the candles.

The whole thing over in five minutes!

Instead of being late for an 11:00 service, she had arrived at the tail of one that had started at 10:00. "About right for someone who hasn't been in a church for a long time," she told a girl who came to greet her. But she liked the gilded space and the procession with the cross—and the congregation's shout in response to the blessing had made her feel unexpectedly joyful.

A pale luminous angel standing in the last window caught her eye on the way out, so that she blinked and looked a second time. The flesh shone opal, with veins that turned to white fire as the sun brightened.

She wondered what sort of creature he was, this sexless, radiant figure, pieced together from burning gems and—what?—raw energy? Even the string of leaves around the neck seemed to shine with the essence of first spring days, cold yet sunny, as if they would soon sprout and vine the world with green. His every step might ignite the ground with strange, otherworldly vigor.

He was as pure and flame-like as a sword.

I might be afraid of you, if you were real and not a made thing, she thought. *What would you tell me? That I exist, maybe? Could it be that simple? Would you say, "I am other than you, utterly alien. And I demand—"*

Her thoughts broke off; it was her turn at the door.

"Cynthia Sorrel," she said.

"Ah, the painter. You must come again." Hale Wren clasped her hand. "Lydia has talked about you. We need an artistic soul like yours."

"I'm not really a churchgoer," she confessed.

"But you're a pursuer of mystery," he said, not letting go of her fingers, "an artist, are you not? I've spent my life in pursuit of one mystery."

She couldn't help smiling at him, though the question "an artist, are you not?" rang strangely on her ear and seemed to lead only to doubt and trouble.

Am I? Is there anything genuine left in me?

She remembered the boy in the grove and the longing that had awakened and seemed to hurt her very heart. Perhaps something remained. This bony-looking man with the penetrating gray eyes seemed to challenge her. *An artist, are you not?*

"Yes," she said, not knowing whether she assented to another visit or to being an artist or simply to the grandeur and perhaps folly of a lifelong chase of mystery.

"Hale, you've got hold of Cynthia! She's here—I'm so glad." Lydia took her arm and guided her away from the church. "I hope my husband was nice to you. He can be disconcerting; it's this terrible instinct he has for going to the heart of things. Dangerous. Like a blade let out of its scabbard. The old priest, Father Martin, was softer. He helps with the service now and then."

Lydia adjusted the balance of her hat and added, "I still don't grasp whether to admire Hale Wren or to consider him rude."

"He's quite all right," Cynthia said, "or quite right, or something—he made me wonder, anyway, and that's more than most people do."

"Yes, he does manage that. Rather formidably, I'd say."

Though the grass was still soaked, the two women wandered in the graveyard, Lydia pointing out the graves of the famous novelist, the historian, the poet famous in his day, the village founder, and the rector who planted churches in the wilderness, his wife and baptismal bowl perched behind him on the horse. She tapped on the stones with a rolled-up church bulletin as if to summon their shades from rest.

"Hat's progressing nicely—"

It was Andrew, calling across the graves. Teddy stood at his elbow, neat in a gray suit with a tapestry vest.

Must be Teddy's trademark, vests. Cynthia's gaze went to Andrew, his mane of hair pushed by the breeze. The gray topcoat draped over his shoulders flew back like wings.

"No thanks to you." Lydia stamped her feet as she gained the walk.

"If you must know, I'm bringing my contribution next week," Andrew said.

"So he can amaze the populace." Teddy threw out his arms, and Cynthia was amused to see a gaudy pattern of cell phones on the vest.

"I can hardly wait to see what it is this time," Lydia said.

"No worry—I know the rules—no more taxidermy. Considering a potted plant this time." Andrew wore a look

Cynthia remembered from their first meeting, as if he were about to laugh.

"'Mock contrite' butters no Yankee parsnips with me!" Lydia took Teddy's arm and walked off with him toward the parish hall. "Come for coffee," she called back to the others, but Cynthia only waved, thinking more than ever what a Tweedledee the elder Wild appeared. It must be the vests.

"How's the roof?"

Andrew's eyes gave her a jolt of blue, making Cynthia think of the figure in the scrub and the way his glance had struck at her.

"Mr. Gimble said he'd finish tomorrow, after he picks up some more slate."

"And nothing else has gone amiss?"

"Last night I dreamed about a water dragon in the shape of the Sea House doorknocker," she told him. "How's that?" The beast had lurked under the hill, waiting to devour the favorite cousin and maul little Izzie, a tagalong wisp who hadn't had the sense to run away.

"A bit unusual."

"It's the cottage that does it, I guess."

He laughed and said, "The gatehouse gives people peculiar thoughts." He made it sound perfectly natural for a place to seep into dreams. Perhaps he knew, living in Sea House. "You could've been dreaming of the salamanders. They're as near to dragons as anything on earth, I suppose—too tiny, but said to live in fire. If a doorknocker that goes jigging around the countryside and hops into an unsuspecting dream is your worst problem—"

37

"Then I must be fine," she broke in.

"I'd say so." He rocked on his heels as though he hadn't a care.

She surveyed him. "You seem to have…a gift for joy." It wasn't that he had no troubles. But she could feel the warmth and cheer of the man like a mortal sunshine. *A woman could bask in light like that,* she thought. *Could be at ease.*

When he didn't respond, Cynthia felt her tentative sense of belonging dissolve. "I'm sorry—was that too personal?"

He gave a shake of the head. "It's a compliment that I probably don't deserve, and so I thank you."

His smile returned slowly, until she felt comfortable and found herself talking about how the boy had materialized on the other side of the creek, how there was something unusual about him, and how he stood staring, shirtless in the cold morning mist.

"I don't want a trespasser to drive you from the gatehouse." Andrew rapped the tip of his umbrella on the walk for emphasis.

"Oh, I don't think he meant any harm."

"You weren't afraid, then?" He looked closely at her.

"No, not exactly. I was startled."

"Perhaps it was an apparition."

He didn't mean it, Cynthia thought; Andrew might be laughing at her, or at himself, or at past-haunted Cooper Patent—the creaky houses and the tales left over from the eighteenth and nineteenth centuries.

"Lots of villagers claim to have bumped into ghosts," he added.

"I don't think so. But the sight felt full of meaning, though I don't know how to read it." Cynthia gazed at Andrew, as if she might find the answer in the blue of his eyes. "A long time has passed since my life seemed like a story tinged with mystery, worth the reading," she said slowly, "and I rather marvel that it can feel that way again."

He reached for her hand, and she let him lift it and examine the palm. She was trembling slightly, more from the surprising admission of something so intimate than from the chill. It was as if Hale Wren's question had unlocked an inward door.

"Here, see? The old gimcrack fortune-teller says, 'it sounds like a picture to me.' Maybe that's what it means."

Cynthia gently withdrew her hand from his.

"And I thought that life- and love-lines were all."

"Oh, they're nonsense. The fortune-teller cheats and reads the heart, I suppose." Andrew shifted to watch the wind threshing the yellow maples across the street in Cooper Park.

"And what does he read in mine?"

"All a mystery," he said.

She followed his gaze to where a skein of yellow leaves twisted in the breeze.

"A mystery." There it was again—something to decipher.

He glanced down at her.

"Except the picture, of course. You'd have to paint it if you wanted to find out what the boy means."

"Everybody's out to tell me what to do today," she exclaimed, thinking about the priest's words and even Lydia, saying that her husband always went to the heart of the matter.

And the boy in the grove, most of all: what was he saying? There was a challenge in his look. She could almost see an answer, like something invisible swarming and taking shape in the air.

"Look," she cried out, delighted. "Would you look! The first snowflakes of winter."

Will o' the Wisp

How did I get so busy?"
"I certainly can't tell. It creeps up, doesn't it? You think village life ought to be all dilly-dallying and picking flowers, but it's not." Lydia's fork clinked against the dessert plate. She and Cynthia were having lunch in the gatehouse.

"Well, I like having too many things to do." Cynthia spooned up a last dollop of cream, feeling happy that Teddy had commissioned portraits of himself and Andrew, even though the latter declared the house already overrun with ugly old ancestors. Still, he was letting it happen.

"Now that you've been coerced into the village art guild, you'll soon be browbeaten into more. And if you're not overbooked by then, you could try being Hale's assistant wife. He needs one, I'm afraid." Lydia looked at her watch and jumped up. "I'm off to meet him at the hospital, my friend."

"My friend," Cynthia echoed, liking the idea.

Yes, it was good to be tugged from her routines. One day she had driven to the city and replenished her watercolor pans and papers, but an unforeseen shyness had come over her as she added linen canvas, oil paints, gesso, linseed oil, and varnish—the last an optimistic touch, as she wouldn't need it for six months or more after a picture was completed. Foss Norlander, from whom she had been buying for decades, calculated her purchases without comment, but after helping to stow the packages in her trunk, he presented her with a box carved with an interlace of waves, fish, and birds.

"My homemade gift," he had said, giving her a kiss on the cheek. "You have done a big thing, and I take notice. Next time, bring some images to show me."

In the week after her return, she took photographs of the brothers for reference, though she hoped they would be doing plenty of sittings at Sea House. But she was making other plans as well. Crossing the stream, she cut samples from shrubs and trees and stuffed them into jars in her studio. She made sketches of the forest. Secretly, she began the underpainting of a large oil, though she had decided that she wanted the boy not in a scene of autumn but in a simpler, greener setting. It bothered her, altering the memory, as if she were inserting something fantastic into the world.

"But it's natural, isn't it? The leaves will be green again, and if the ones I paint aren't right, I can do them again in spring." She won the argument with herself and kept on painting.

Lydia's hat had gone on display in the parish hall, its brim loaded with baubles. Iz had added a fishing lure with its barbs corked, Teddy a rose made from a rattlesnake's skin, and Andrew a toy-sized Tiffany vase with thumb-dents and a note packed inside that read "love to the formidable Lydia Wren, with apologies for the peacock."

In Cooper Patent Park, the maples were moated in pools of yellow leaves.

Minor snows had arrived and melted. The great deluge was still to come, Teddy told her, warning that they always got more bad weather than any of the surrounding towns. Evidently it was the lake's fault.

One unexpectedly warm afternoon, she was painting outside when Iz walked around the corner of the cottage and saw the picture that Cynthia had wanted to keep secret.

"Sorry I was in such a foul mood when you showed up a while ago." She ducked her head, lighting the butt of a cigarette.

"Hello, Iz." Cynthia faced away from the painting, half blocking the image, and set down her palette and brush.

"All hooks and needles sometimes," Iz muttered. It seemed to be an apology.

"It's fine. It's all right," Cynthia said.

Iz blew smoke from her nose in a short, sharp burst. "Who's that?"

"Oh, I don't know."

"Nobody I've met," Iz declared.

"I'm not surprised. Just a boy. I'm on the second layer now; you can't tell much so far." Cynthia wanted to protect him from prying, tender and incomplete as he was, and she felt a wave of dislike for the other woman. She shook her head, as if to dislodge bad humors.

It wasn't fair to picture Iz as a fire-dwelling imp—not when she hardly knew her—to make up a shadow person and call it by name as though the portrait were genuine. *All hooks and needles? That would hurt.*

"You've already started a picture of Theodore, I hear." Iz said the name with a note of scorn. She picked up a tube of *Chinese Lake* and set it down again.

"You didn't see it?" Cynthia suspected that she would've barged over as soon as word reached the gardener's cottage.

Iz picked a shred of tobacco from her tongue. "Teddy wouldn't let me in the door," she said, lighting another cigarette.

She tossed the match, and the two women watched it fall, blackening and writhing before the head turned ashen and sent up a last gray signal of life.

"Why not?"

Iz took a drag. For some seconds she didn't answer, and only slowly did thin revenants of smoke crawl from her nostrils. A cough ratcheted deep in her throat. "Ash. Smoke.

He won't have it. Of course, they burn logs in the fireplaces. So it's not really that."

"Maybe wood smoke's not the same as tobacco smoke." Cynthia walked to the brink of the stream, and her mind skipped across the slash of the bed and wandered in the leafless grove.

"Smoke is smoke, I say."

Harold. The name sprang up before she remembered the bold little picture-book boy who climbed castles and scaled the moon, drawing as he went. He would have thrown a bridge over the gulch and chased after the figure in the scrub. For Iz, he'd whip up a machine that drank smoke and expelled cumulus, or give her a silly hat like Lydia's and big shoes and a red nose.

"*Harold and the Purple Crayon.* Did you ever read that book?"

Iz didn't hear.

Cynthia couldn't make the world over, or discern anything through haze but this splintered, maimed person. Was she more than bristling sharp points, more than needles without eyes to see? Harold could've drawn a banner over the snarl of hair and scribbled *PITY* on it. With that much help, maybe she could feel sorry.

"Are you wool-gathering?"

Cynthia wheeled about and said, "Guess that's exactly what I'm doing."

"Here, I was supposed to bring these a long time ago, but I'd misplaced them. There's at least one key for each door, plus some to cupboards in the kitchen and cellar." Iz plunked the keys into Cynthia's hand.

45

She hefted the iron ring. "Don't they look wonderful? I'll enjoy poking around."

And when she saw the boy a second time, it was thanks to Iz and because of the keys she had brought. Cynthia had climbed onto a chair and was thrusting one shaft after another into a locked cabinet by a window.

Glimpsing the boy through the wavy panes, she let go of the ring, and the keys clashed onto the counter. She didn't stop to pick it up but darted for a jacket and flung open the nearest door. Already he was moving away, visible as flicks of color behind the trees. Shirtless, again: wasn't it far too cold? Perhaps teenage boys ran hot, the hormones of puberty surging in their veins.

Cynthia slipped on wet leaves by the creek and grabbed at a root to slow her fall. The crooked thing burned her palm as she slammed feet first onto an outcropping of slate, reeled, and kicked off, jumping from stone to stone. The water gurgled in its channel, just deep enough to wet her shoes and socks. Seizing an overhanging bough, she hauled herself up the other side and knelt, panting, at the brink.

"I've lost him…"

Beyond the lake road, something passing behind a cluster of maples made a stutter of white. She pursued it, veering between stripling trees whose tiny last leaves were like flecks from a far-flung spatter of blood. At the macadam she bolted across and plunged into a ravel of vines.

"No," she whispered, "no."

The boy had already reached the top of the hill.

On the climb, she refused to pause when the saliva in her mouth grew metallic and breath sawed unpleasantly in her throat. Nor did she give up when the slope proved only the first in a waving line.

The glimmer retreated before her like a will o' the wisp until the flitter of pale skin went out like a snuffed candle.

"He's gone."

Cynthia gained a low ridge where the trees were hardwood, set wide apart in drifts of leaves. She walked slowly, shivering as her damp skin cooled. Looking about, she realized that the boy had led her toward Sea House. She could make out the roof and the place where one wing merged with earth.

"Ah!" The syllable made a single, twanging note in the cold.

The boy was cresting the flank above Sea House, swinging lightly along the steepest part. And he was wholly bare! He would get hypothermia and die in the woods, Cynthia thought, unless a fire was waiting for him. She remembered the streakers of her girlhood who had raced naked through the streets in protest of rules and war and middle-aged sobriety.

So perhaps he was fine, headed toward warmth.

A threadlike cut on her cheek smarted with sweat and oozed a few crimson tears. The scrape on her palm began to throb. If she climbed down and walked to Sea House, the Wild brothers would ferry her to the cottage. Andrew's ratty old Jaguar was parked by the front walk.

"No, don't think I'll ask," she murmured. She didn't want them to see her like this, hands and face soiled, hair tumbled, and burrs hitched to her jacket.

Her feet had gone numb in the drenched shoes, and she stripped off her wet socks and crammed them under a tree root. Unsure of finding her way home, Cynthia determined to follow the Sea House drive to the lake road. She regained the creek by following the sound of trickling and discovered that the water spilled from a pool dammed with sticks and mud. A beaver slammed its tail against the surface; the slap made her jump. Just as she spied the soaked head and the water receding behind the body in a widening V, the animal dipped and was gone. Cynthia waited, jigging in place and rubbing her arms for warmth, but it didn't return.

Wary of the pent-up waters, she crossed a hundred yards below the lodge, teetering on stepping-stones. The final pitch of land was steeper than the climb from the gatehouse, tilting her forward until she scrambled low and clutched at trees and stems. When a burrow trapped her foot, she tripped and fell at full-length on the grass. She was glad to clamber the last few yards and reach the flat lane; if it had been warmer, she would have kicked off her shoes.

Cynthia bent to gently massage her ankle. *Might've pulled a ligament.* The pain wasn't too bad, but she limped and wished herself at the gatehouse.

The leafy sprays that had clogged the lane in August were bare. She passed easily through their ravel of limbs, her thoughts elsewhere, gathering around the naked boy like a garment.

Funny, she'd never before considered any danger. What might he have done, when his glance alone had been a blow? Perhaps he was like the stream, pent but liable to hurl itself outward, destroying whatever lay in its path. Perhaps his fists would go berserk, hammering—

"Whatever have you been doing?" Andrew craned from the car window, the wind fooling with his hair, pushing locks into his eyes.

Like a child found out in mischief, Cynthia put up her hands to cover her face.

"You look somewhat like a leafy Eve—only different," he remarked, easing the Jaguar forward. "A denizen of nature. Get in. I promise not to look at you."

Half sorry, half glad, she limped to the door as he reached across to help.

"Oops, sorry—I couldn't help peeking."

"Hah." Inside, the Jaguar's buttery leather seats and burled wood belied the exterior, with its holes where chrome and hood ornament should have been and its half-sanded metal. She closed her eyes, not caring if he had seen. It was delicious to lean back and feel herself melting into the cushions.

"It suits you. Being flushed and bedraggled, I mean."

"Thanks."

"*Bedraggled* is not quite right. *Tousled*, I think it is."

Cynthia nestled against the seat. *Tousled*. That one she would ignore. The whips of hedge dragged along the car, making a long *scrrreeeek*.

"Your poor car."

"You should have seen Teddy's old roadster. Scratched but beautiful. Then Izzie got drunk and totaled it. Messed up her face and arms."

"Oh." *So that's what happened.*

"I might give those a trim, if I ever finish up the car—won't hurt the paint job now. But we like them this way."

"Wild."

"It tends to keep out unwanted visitors. So tell me, where have you been gadding about to pick up all those hitchhikers and make yourself so pink in the face?"

Tiny green triangles had stuck to her jeans. "What a lot of beggar's lice," she said, surveying her legs.

"Yes," he said, "and what were you doing in the forest?"

She sighed. "I went after the boy. The one I saw before. Who appeared on the far side of the creek."

"And I suppose he wasn't interested in being caught."

"It was a fool thing to do."

"Maybe."

"He outpaced me. I don't think we were ever matched, because after I lost sight of him momentarily and paused to rest, he made it to the trees above Sea House."

"He's fast." Andrew gave her a sharp glance. "And going nowhere civilized—there's nothing much beyond but woods."

"I wonder if he wanted me to chase him. He looked back twice. Like he was daring me on, maybe."

"And you hunted him through 'hollow lands and hilly lands' and never met him." He reached across and pressed her hand. "That's good for us. You might have disappeared."

Cynthia gave a mere twitch of a shiver.

"He was naked. I didn't realize it until I saw him on the slope above the house. Last time I thought he had no shirt."

"How extraordinary. In weather like this." Andrew had stopped at the lake road without attempting to cross, and his fingers tapped at the wheel. She noticed that his nails were cut close and scrupulously clean. Her own were packed with dirt from the banks of the creek.

"Yes. Jaybird-bare."

"Was he…" Andrew paused and looked her full in the face. "Was there anything ghostly about him?"

The ankle had begun to throb. Cynthia closed her eyes to focus on the image of a boy vanishing.

"Your cousin who was lost in the hill—"

"Mad, isn't it? To even think so for a second." A spatter of drops struck the windshield; he drove on.

"I don't know. Maybe." Her eyes watered from pain, and she blotted them with the back of her hand. They felt like tears for the lost cousin.

Nearly every street in Cooper Patent claimed a haunted pier glass or a room enchanted to cold or a picture that could not be moved without upsetting a poltergeist. Only the day before, Lydia had declared the village "rife with spirits." Later, Cynthia met the Wrens on the sidewalk, and the three paused by a broken wall where the village's kicking Mohawk chief was buried. "What nonsense!" Hale had cried, adding more quietly that he didn't mind so much. "All mystery that draws the heart is of use," he murmured, the words cryptic even now. What did it mean to be of use, and how could the story of a ghost be so—or a picture, for that matter?

"No," Cynthia said. "He was as real as you or me. His eyes were unsettling. Potent. He was singular-looking."

"And naked."

"Yes. But solid, you know, like a person. Not a dream or a spirit."

Andrew gazed past the lake road toward Glimmerglass, as if still mulling over what she had seen. The lake, ever changeable, floated like a silvery ghost behind the trees. A model T puttered by on its way to a show at one of the museums. Cynthia was almost home, with a jog down the road and a dash through the gate remaining.

"There's no telling," he said, and let the car roll forward. "Shall I take a look at the repairs to the roof? And you ought to let me tape up that ankle. I've got a first aid kit in the trunk. In case I meet up with an injured tree nymph."

A handful of raindrops had left the arch glinting, and a few sparkling crystals fell from a griffin's beak.

"All right." Cynthia drew her wrenched ankle closer to the seat. He had noticed. "Why don't you come in?"

Snow on Snow

The ankle worsened the next day, and it was more than a week before she could move about without hobbling.

"It's a good thing you didn't walk all the way home," Andrew said. He and Teddy presented her with an old blackthorn cane, and they brought dinner for several nights running, though she protested.

The Wrens came by with a half-bushel of pears and another of a sour apple good for baking—or for eating, if you had a taste for the difficult. Hale caught sight of the painted boy, propped in the middle of her studio, and stood staring until Lydia found him there and led him away.

"When I was over at Sea House, I liked Teddy's portrait very much—and the one you've begun of Andrew. But I didn't realize you were as good as this. It's wonderful, really wonderful." His eyes rested on Cynthia's face for a too-long glance, so that she blushed and reached for her cane.

Even Iz showed up with a shepherd's pie that, when the foil was removed, smelled disturbingly of smoke, as if cigarettes might have been absentmindedly stubbed out in the dish. Cynthia set the casserole to air on a stump behind the cottage, where it was later eaten by a party of raccoons.

The snows began in earnest that week, and by the time she could walk freely, the ground was a foot deep in white. She drove through nets of fine, blowing crystal on her first outing—to Sea House to finish Teddy's portrait and work on the one of Andrew. While confined to the gatehouse, she had completed her fall commissions, all based on photographs.

She didn't mind the hack jobs so much now; she would be painting in oils on a regular basis. Perhaps she would give up the watercolor commissions in time. A friend of Teddy's had admired his portrait, now hanging in a hallway at Sea House, and passed her name to some of the wealthy families along the lake. Meanwhile, Teddy had suggested to Lydia that she write one of her columns for the paper about Cynthia's Sea House portraits. Yes, she would soon have plenty to do, even though Teddy had more than tripled the price when asked about her fees.

"You're well worth it. And they can afford that amount." He looked rather smug. But perhaps it was the plum-colored vest with the embroidered gold crowns that made him so pleased with himself, because he smoothed the cloth over his belly and gave the fabric a quick pat as he spoke. "Besides, we need to keep you out of trouble, don't we?"

"I'm in your debt," she told him, but he only shrugged.

"The least I could do. You gave us a great bargain. It was really unfair."

It hadn't been, though. Cynthia was long out of practice with oils and even now felt some uncertainty about her painting of the boy, though it was finished or nearly so. Yet the work had gone well, exceeding her expectations, and so she feared to spoil what she had made. She would let the piece sit for a while and then decide whether it was done. Her model hadn't come back to the opening in the scrub with its backdrop of young trees. Perhaps the weather had kept him away.

Everyone had warned her that the snows would be nothing like the ones she knew. Sure enough, the crystal came down like never-ending weather in a fairy tale. Stars and prisms collected in glittering drifts; from time to time, a sudden slippage and fall from branches made the ever-greens dance in a cloud of bright dust.

Once she glimpsed a human shape reeling through flurries and thought of the boy. Trudging through drifts by the lake road, she saw in the irregular form of a slope the planes of his face, closed and still like a plaster mask, but huge. One day Andrew helped her make a snow maiden,

55

and that night she dreamed of climbing out of bed to peer from a window and see how the figure looked by moonlight. In blue air, the luminous girl and the boy were embracing. Birds pecked at the seed spilled at their feet or perched on shoulders to doze, feathers puffed out and heads tucked under a wing.

It stormed more in the early hours, so in the morning she couldn't tell if the dimples on the surface of the snow marked the site of fresh footprints.

The months slid past like chains of stars along a windowpane. During Advent, Lydia invited her twice to tea—just the two of them. Cynthia was glad; she felt positive that the other woman would be a close friend. At the rectory, she stumbled upon a bedroom where stuffed frogs played the parts of shepherds and kings on pilgrimage to a stable in Bethlehem. Mary was a frog in a blue scarf, Joseph a bearded toad. The little Messiah was a peeper with a fluted gold candy cup behind his head.

"Don't take it wrong, but that's nothing," Lydia confessed, coming up behind her. "You should see us at Easter! We've been doing frog pageants for years."

"How funny. I never would have guessed that Hale could be so silly," Cynthia said. She returned the pale green baby to the manger.

On Christmas Eve she went to church with Teddy and Andrew, singing hymns that took her back to her mother's arms and the scent of cut boughs on the mantle. When a tall acolyte turned his head, she breathed in slowly, her eyes on the profile. No, it wasn't the boy, not at all. Near the end, when not just the altar and the Advent wreath but the whole church was lit by candles—hand-held ones thrust through stiff paper disks—the golden light on hair and skin touched her like enchantment.

"So lovely!"

Hale kissed her on the forehead when she paused at the threshold. His white and purple robes hung down like folded wings.

"I'm glad you came—perfect, wasn't it? Next week, come to lunch on Thursday," Lydia called to her.

Some of the other faces had begun to seem familiar, and a few of them she met again at an immense New Year's party at Sea House, where Iz Hix became very drunk and swayed conspicuously under a chandelier before crumpling onto a faded Persian carpet.

"They can't do without me," she had slurred, just before the fall. Dressed in a narrow satin blouse and black velvet skirt, she resembled nothing so much as a jumble of pick-up sticks in an elegant sack. The rented college-boy bartenders toted her away, slung like a hammock.

Most of the other guests flowed by in a stream of introductions, moving so swiftly that Cynthia couldn't retain the names. Already she was forgetting the warm sense of being a part of something that she had felt at Christmas and was positive that she would never be woven into the life of the village. She would always be a contrary thread moving diagonally across warp and woof.

The town had layers and hierarchies, difficult to grasp. At top were the guardians, inbred and proud, seated like she-dragons on gold. Or so she imagined; she had no way to unlock the permutations of belonging and not belonging.

Even if the mayor presented her with the key to the village in a public ceremony, she would still be unable to get in.

When she felt at her most woebegone, having been snubbed with an astounded look and a refusal to reply by a tallowy personage who was someone of importance at the summer opera house, Andrew found and swept her away.

"Aren't we having fun yet? Are we meshing with the natives?" He steered her into another room and put a glass of champagne in her hand.

"Not quite." But already it wasn't true. She felt his presence like a balm.

"Was it Tristan? Don't pay any attention. He comes off as a cad, but he's nice, once you have a proper introduction. Anyway, he doesn't like strangers much. Nor children, nor people who don't know opera, come to that."

"He was pretty deflating," she admitted.

"The English accent makes the remark seem worse than it is."

"Oh, he didn't have to say a word. In fact, he wouldn't. It was a hackneyed moment out of a Regency romance, when the aristocrat meets a girl with flowers in her hair instead of proper jewels. Naturally, he looked on me and detected a specimen of the lower and less edible orders of crustacea. And in turn, I grasped what it means for someone's lip to curl."

Andrew laughed at this picture of his guest. "I like Tris, but he is a terrible young snob. He would've been pleasant to you, if he'd known that you painted Teddy's portrait—he told me that it was first-rate."

Reaching back to a childhood that relished funny voices, Cynthia dredged up an English accent: "How very foolish of him."

"Yes, it is."

"And I'll wager," she added, "his old man was a costermonger! Though I don't really get what a costermonger is—I just like the sound of it."

"I think it's a sort of peddler. An apple seller, something like that. Eels or cabbages. Sausages. Food, I'm sure. Anyway, Tristan's from Newark. I've heard a few people say that his real name is *Duane*. He was an exchange student in London back in high school, and his voice has never recovered from the revelations of that year."

"Newark!" Cynthia laughed at the thought. *Tristan of Newark.* "I will have to forgive him."

When Andrew took her hand, the contact was like a glittering at the bone. His eyes looked nearly black, the pupils gone large as if to see her better. "How about a dance? Did you know that Sea House has a ballroom? Named *The Emerald Sea Ballroom* by my Aunt Penelope. There's a chamber of every kind in the family labyrinth."

"I'm not much of a dancer." A tickling sensation began in her fingers; she wanted to comb them through his hair. She liked him, though he was old village and she but Johnny-come-lately. And ne'er the twain could be one, as far as she could tell.

"That's all right. I'm not a bad guide."

"I hear—fiddles. Not too close by." A skirling music echoed, as though the door to the maze of tunnels and caverns under the hill had been flung open.

"Big as it is, you'd never find the ballroom without me. We always have somebody to search for and pilot the lost at parties, and once the fellow got tipsy and traipsed around with a gang of dancers half the night. I've always suspected that he got into the hill somehow, though the door was locked. They didn't stumble in until brunch—and told stories about rooms I couldn't begin to identify."

"Sea House is—"

She stopped, conjuring a puzzle of hallways and the forbidden threshold where the house ran wild. Just thinking of the strangeness and magic of the place brought a swell of pleasure.

"What frisky music," she said. "Let's dance."

———

The aftermath of New Year's and Twelfth Night parties was the deep hush of winter, when many of the villagers flew away to southern sun or else hibernated, hunkered close to the hearth. By February, Cynthia wearied of snow and the pall on the sky that promised more and more of the same. During a week of thaw, she wandered the margins of lake and creek. Water seeped through cracks in the ice, gathering into rivulets that sang as they trickled over slabs that, in turn, broke apart and jammed the deep groove of the streambed. Out hiking on the fifth day of warmth, she trailed after a flicker of movement in the dense cover. She paused, feeling uneasy, and as her eyes became used to the shade under the evergreens, she spotted eyes gleaming in the thicket. Three—but three what? One of them swiveled its head, snuffing the air.

"It's all right," Cynthia whispered.

She halted, watched until the shy figures dropped from their upright posture and disappeared, bolting through the brush. On the ground where they had stood, she discovered a few gnawed sticks. The beavers must have tired of huddling in the lodge and gone out, scrounging for food. They had looked like dwarves caught in an act of secrecy. An image of them wearing Teddy's vests popped into her mind: one in mulberry sprinkled with Labradors, one in night-with-stars, and the big one in crowns.

The Painted Boy

*F*at over thin, that's all I know about oil painting in a nutshell." After an hour of reading aloud while Andrew sat for his portrait, Teddy was bustling about the kitchen, making a small drama out of a silver tray and tea with mint from the garden, cut and frozen in the past summer.

"It's good advice," Cynthia called from the butler's pantry, moving over at the sink as Andrew reached around her for the towel. He paused, hand gripping the iron bar, looking down at her.

"She doesn't want to paint in a nutshell," he murmured.

"Silly," she said, and picked up the glass of water she had come for, holding it in the same hand as the wet brush she had brought by accident, lost in thought.

"But what does she want, I wonder?" He let go of the towel and grasped her arm, paying no attention to the brush in her fingers.

"Perhaps I want—"

"You're going to get oil paint on that nice Irish fisherman's sweater." Teddy rapped on the counter with a spoon.

Cynthia smiled at Andrew, her free hand glancing against his. "That would be a beastly shame."

"Right," he said, catching up the towel, "I'd hate to upset an Irish fisherman."

What Andrew wanted remained obscure to Cynthia. Sometimes he appeared merely genial, while at other moments she could sense the fine silk of desire binding them in a dazzling cocoon. She liked him more than she had liked anybody in a long time. That was as much as she let herself think, though he often invited her to stay for tea after a sitting.

Once she had gone to fetch a bundle of sketches left at the door and met him in the shadowy hall. He slipped his arms around her and laid his cheek against her hair, and she stood on tiptoe to press him close. Immediately he stepped back, almost pushing her away.

She had the sensation of being watched and nearly laughed: that Teddy! He was everywhere, it seemed.

But the eyes resting on her were not his.

"That's Marian's portrait," Andrew said. "I didn't realize where—"

"I'm sorry."

"I don't want to go through something like—I promised myself, never again."

Had the two been happy, before sickness dismantled a marriage? Teddy had suggested that Marian became more difficult over time. Unsure whether Andrew's words meant his wife's illness and death or marriage with its risk of loss, she said only, "I can understand that."

"Losing her—first as the person she used to be and later on the ebbing and dying..."

A draft touched the nape of Cynthia's neck and made her tremble. Glancing away, she saw a cluster of icicles pressed against the windowpanes; pale and phantasmal in the gloom, they reminded her that Cooper Patent was a village pestered with ghosts. She had the sense that three of them—not two—stood in the hallway and that the painted figure divided the living and meant to keep them apart.

Afterward, the image of the dead woman's eyes in the dusk stayed with her. She could no longer pass through the front rooms of Sea House without remembering that Andrew had had a wife and meant never to suffer such a loss again.

———

Teddy had mentioned that twelve of the pictures at the museum were on loan from Sea House, and one day

Cynthia invited Lydia to come along and take a look. Inside Fenimore House, she forgot the lowering clouds and cold of February. The first three pictures were beauties—a pencil sketch of Cora's death for *Scene from The Last of the Mohicans* by Thomas Cole, a painting of a cataract wrapped in luminous mist attributed to John Frederick Kensett, and an oil by Frederick Church titled *Scene with Aurora Borealis*, its moody lake tentatively identified as Glimmerglass.

"Ridiculously romantic." Lydia had made the circuit of the room and now returned to her side.

"As lavish as some people's hats," Cynthia murmured. She had paused in front of a painting of Sea House streaked by rays from a red and orange sunset.

"Bombastic, aren't they?" Lydia touched her hair as if recalling the weight of her fundraiser hat. "But I like them."

"You ought to, I guess, being bound to a priest." Cynthia turned toward a large landscape of rocks and dark passages. "The Hudson River Valley painters were passionate sorts, and Asher Durand said that he and his painter friends meant to show the work of God in visible creation. Something like that."

"I just didn't realize that Eden would be quite so opulent," Lydia said, trailing after her.

"The wilderness must've seemed an awfully big and scary place. Lots of torrents and gorges." Cynthia leaned close, almost touching the frame. "This one's listed as from Sea House and the only known painting by somebody named Judith Pomeroy Wild."

"Strange, isn't it?"

"I wonder—it's described as 'possibly Howe Caverns.' But maybe it's not. Maybe this is what the Sea House hill looks like inside." The picture was cracked, as though the painter hadn't observed the "fat on thin" of Teddy's maxim. Pouring from a floor like ice, bluish light revealed the rounded ceiling of a cave and walls suggestive of a maze, zigzagging into the dark. A few shafts of sunlight glowed in the distance, and a female figure could be seen scaling what looked a moraine below one of them.

"If it is, there must be openings in the hill." Lydia drifted on to the next picture, a canvas of tear-streaked cliffs and storm clouds and dripping foliage, with a toy settler and Indian off in one corner, passing a pipe between them.

"Maybe I'll climb up and look when the snows disappear."

"If they do," returned Lydia.

Cynthia trailed after her friend. "Don't they always? Or is there something about Cooper Patent you need to tell me?"

"I lose faith in spring every winter," Lydia said, "so I'm bowled over when the snow finally melts and the sun comes back. You know what I love? Snowdrops. The pure insanity of them, blooming in the dark underneath the snow."

"Brave little things," Cynthia murmured, her gaze resting on the tiny figures lost in their romantic, chasmal landscape.

———

After that, the cold came down hard until March, when the lake began melting, though the ice fishing shanties were still up. Once more the creek began to percolate and sing. Glimmerglass would be clear by May, except for some floating islands that might linger in shady reaches near shore. Though she had delayed the last touches on the second Wild portrait, Cynthia no longer had a reason to go to Sea House. She soon missed her afternoon visits and suspected that Andrew was avoiding her—the cadence of his "promised myself, never again" coming back to her when she considered him. Occasionally she went to church, where he was as warm as ever, but she seldom met him otherwise. Once she saw his rusty car turn around near the gate, as if he'd been coming to see her but changed his mind.

"You're getting older," she observed, staring into the mirror. "Time to give up on dreams." But she didn't believe it. Inside, she was no older than the naked boy who had glanced over his shoulder as he vanished into the trees above Sea House.

She clambered about the stream, painting watercolors of the spray flying from rocks and the quaint shapes of ice gnawed by the flow. At night, cold sealed the streams, and frost ferns etched the leaded panes.

One afternoon Teddy dropped by to look at some of her new drawings and watercolors.

"Now this is good," he announced, picking through her portfolio. "You do your own frames, don't you? Can I show some of these to Sybil at the gallery downtown? She's a friend of mine. And I could probably sell some at Moon Gate."

"In your little shop of treasures? Sure, if you like. I wasn't going to send images of these to the printer. I only do that with my tourist pictures. I'm not really looking for a gallery, but a few local outlets would be fine."

"Why don't you paint Sea House in watercolor for me? I need a gift for Andrew."

"If you think he'd like that," she said slowly.

"Yes, I do." Teddy inspected her. "He can be a hermit, now and then. There's plenty of room for that at Sea House. Andrew's heading up a brand new project for the museum, and he goes to his room when he gets home—misses dinner half the time."

"What sort of project?"

"A thing about village history and local writers and artists. He's always laboring on some pet plan—adding on a bit of consulting here, a speech to curators there. The endless ocean of roof always has to be repaired and the stones re-mortared. Me, I'd rather stay snug at home and let the walls crumble."

So perhaps Andrew's absence wasn't about her. Perhaps it was a mood.

"You're both busy, from what I hear," she said.

"Can't believe it all. Somebody else does the selling and bookkeeping for the shop, and the buying is enjoyable enough." Teddy shuffled the paintings together and slipped them into the portfolio.

"Maybe it's my fault if you haven't seen him," he added. "I might've mentioned something you said about hibernating to paint."

"I don't recall," she said.

"Maybe Andrew thought it was a message. If so, I'll have to correct that impression. How about tea?"

"Sure! A grand idea."

It was hard to remember the way she'd felt about Theodore Wild at first: that he was a bit standoffish, that he didn't like her to spend time with his brother. Now he felt like an ally. He had helped her cling to the spot and begin to make a living, one that felt more meaningful than the thousands of prints that had been sold in her name. Perhaps she'd never be able to give up that income, but she could put the hack jobs in a place many steps below the portraits and the painting of the boy. Barring some minor fiddling, the most luminous and beautiful thing she had ever done was finished.

"If I never do anything else," she told Lydia, "I will have done this."

She'd had such dreams as a girl. To think that all her castles in the air and talent had come down to the anomaly of one nigh-perfect painting, when she'd imagined rank on rank of pictures sailing out into the world. She no longer had the slightest concern about the realm of museums and city galleries, or about what was admired. Nor did she ever recall the years of art school, or the awards stowed in a cardboard box. She had fastened her heart on this one image, and it had resurrected a joy that she had forgotten.

The Spring Freshet

When April blew in, the creek became a jumble of fractured ice. Its loud music woke Cynthia early in the mornings and sang her to sleep at night.

Andrew came by unexpectedly and apologized for interrupting her work. "Teddy said that you were laboring on a large painting and didn't want visitors."

"Oh! That's too bad. He knew that wasn't right. And said that he'd make sure you knew," Cynthia said. "Told him I was not a hermit. But I guess he forgot. He told me that you'd been too busy on a project to see anybody."

"That's not so!" He sat down in the wingback by the fire and rummaged through his pockets. "Teddy can be a rather annoying housemate. Sometimes he gets everything wrong."

"I'm sorry," she said, wondering for an instant whether Teddy could have gotten everything wrong on purpose.

"Me too. I'll have to have a word with my elder half-brother. But let's not worry about that now."

He offered her a taffeta-covered box, faded to a washed-out pink. "Lydia told me that your birthday is this week. I found this in some papers yesterday and thought of you because the colors seemed right. It belonged to my maternal grandmother."

Tucked into satin was an emerald and pearl ring.

"It's lovely." Astonished, she tilted the stone to the light, admiring the old-fashioned setting. "But how can I accept a piece of jewelry that's so valuable—shouldn't it belong to your children?"

"I thought of you," he repeated. He then got up and took his leave, mentioning something about a meeting at the museum.

As she watched the spattered car swerve onto the lake road, the ring lay heavy in her hand. She did not know what to conclude. Was nothing readable and clear? Neither the man nor Cooper Patent made sense at the moment. Mud season was upon the district, the snow sinking and forming big crystals, dirty where they met the ground. She stored the ring inside Foss Norlander's box and planned to return it to Andrew when she saw him next. At least he knew that she had never wanted him to keep away. But he didn't come back. The world continued mixed, water and land slopping together; now and then a brilliantly sunny day would melt a foot of snow.

On a dazzling afternoon, Cynthia flung open the seven doors of her house and mopped the slate in the parlor and the oak boards and last of all the fireplaces. She surveyed the buckets of filthy water with satisfaction, tossing their contents next to a garden bed where bulbs had sent up tiny green minarets and made a fanciful city among crystal hills.

She shook out her hair, brushed cobwebs from her jeans, and retrieved the pink taffeta box.

What did he mean by the ring—too much or too little?

The band slipped into place and fit perfectly. *Spring's on the way,* she thought. *This very day the sap must have wakened and begun to rise.* The emerald glittered on her finger.

Lured from an open door and toward the creek, drawn by the water's tune, she saw *him* and held still. The boy was standing in front of the grove of saplings. Again she had the sense of his gaze as almost brutal. He was telling her something.

What? She mouthed the word, her eyes fixed to his. The frantic song of meltwater was the only answer, though he didn't look away. She drew closer and thought of crossing the stream once more, though the banks were a slough of mud and ice.

As though he had read her mind, the boy put out a hand. *Stop.* She paused, and he gave a little push with his palm. Wind lifted her hair, nudging, as if urging her; she heard a roar. His head jerked toward the road, and she followed his gaze: already churned to foam, a burst of water juggled rocks and trees and jolted along the streambed.

The creek surged above the bank—the boy was gone—and she flashed away, her feet sliding on patches of ice, past the cottage with its seven doors thrown wide, past the firs, and through the gateway with its stone pedestals for ironwork arch and griffins. A wave tangled with her feet, slammed her to the ground. She picked herself up and raced on in deepening water; gaining the lake road, she jogged on a glaze of muddy liquid until she came to dry pavement.

There she panted, hands on muddy knees, and surveyed the invasion of her domain. The stream had flown through the cottage and out the other side, making a shallow lake of the lawn. For an instant she saw the flooded grounds as magical—the reflective surface gleaming like a jewel, the cottage like a moated castle.

"All my things," she whispered.

Though the high waters were already subsiding and draining out the doors, many of her pictures and the upholstered furniture might be ruined, even from such a brief soaking. Had the tide overthrown her tables, broken what was breakable? She dreaded the thought, recalling that when she had moved here, the chance of flood hadn't seemed like such a risk. Less than a year ago, loss had been nothing to her. *Just stuff,* she thought, giving a one-sided smile. Such a quick, fierce dousing wouldn't ruin everything, surely. Old photographs, family possessions: those she couldn't replace.

Cynthia squatted at the edge, watching, until she remembered the painting of the boy and sprang up. She dashed off, heels kicking up spray, slowing as she reached the lake around the house. Chunks of ice, twigs, and leaf litter bobbled on the surface, and last year's flattened grass shone green through the meltwater. Cold lapped against her legs.

Once a pair of small red dragons made her pause. Salamanders from the cellar! Having struck the safety of a tree, they now groped upward and, like two drenched flames, sank into fissures of bark.

Inside, the flood was everywhere, though already the depth had sunk to only five or six inches. The line of the watermark showed that the tide hurled through the open doors must have crested at about three feet. She told herself that it could have been much worse, that perhaps it was best that the doors had been free to let the flood in and out again. She slopped down the hall, rescuing a gilt-framed photograph, a set of overturned nesting tables, and a doll-sized dresser that had belonged to her mother. When she reached the studio, she realized that it had taken the full force of the surge. Drawings together with miniver, sable, and bristle brushes floated on foot-deep water. Collecting her flotsam, she dumped it onto a worktable.

The old map chests full of sketches were safe, but anything half-finished had been torn away, the paints pitched out the door and scattered. Crouching, she groped for what she could salvage. Her hand, blind in the murk, closed on a tube of *Caput Mortuum*. She stared at the dripping tube as if at a message she could read before straightening up and scanning the walls and floor of her studio.

The painting!

She hadn't even dreamed that it might have vanished. Water damage and scratches she could deal with, but not loss.

Cynthia waded back outside and sloshed along the north side of the house, scanning the shadows for a patch of canvas. It could be anywhere between the walls and the shore—could even be in the lake, she realized. And perhaps, if face down, it could fill with water and sink.

"I'll swim if I have to," she said, head bent, as if warning the opaque waters.

She skittered through the yard, twice stumbling to her knees but pushing off again. Discolored where the creek had tumbled its cargo, Glimmerglass was sprinkled with uprooted saplings, dead leaves, and a lone pink plastic Frisbee. Nothing like a picture floated on the waves.

Sticks and stones clogged the mouth of the stream. With unslakable invention, the water continued to murmur its story and find fresh paths into the lake.

"The only thing I ever did that was any good!"

She hardly noticed that she was drenched and cold but crawled onto a heap of debris, peering through gaps, and began to work her way up the heavily pouring creek, poking into the depths with a stick. Nothing. Not until she came within a hundred yards of the house did she glimpse the oval of the boy's face in a deep pool. A mass of wood had forced much of the pell-mell plummet into a nearby channel, although innumerable fingerlets of water felt their way between and over logs.

The banks had been sheared away, so Cynthia climbed downward until she couldn't find footing and abruptly sat, digging her nails into the muck for purchase until the steep wall collapsed, and she smashed sideways into meltwater.

Bubbles shot from her mouth as a branch raked her side. She surfaced, choking and splashing, with clay squeezed in her fists. Something about the clay, soft as raw hanks of flesh in her hands, made the thought of her own death come home to her. Fright was in her, its iron and frost, along with the nightmare of being overrun by a tumult of wood and water. Blood made a jagged path down her ribs. Cold tightened its grip until she gasped.

But she wouldn't climb up; she wouldn't crawl back home in fear. She would claim the boy.

Gingerly she extended her legs, pedaling until her feet found an uneasy perch on the creek bed, and reached for him. With a jerk, the canvas escaped from the grip of mud, though it didn't float to the top as she had expected.

Millais' painting of the drowned Ophelia came into Cynthia's mind as she looked at the boy's heartbreaking, beautiful face and at the white hands glowing under water that was spring clear in places but deepened to coal and blackened emerald in others. Strands of dissolved loam swirled across his chest. She plunged her arms into ice cold and grappled with the canvas, struggling against earth and roots and the weight of water.

An answer to a question she hadn't known to ask, memory and desire rose in her like a fountain and then a

76

flood that ravished: the boy's backward glance from the hill; the receding shape, half-hidden in trees; Andrew, leaning with his hand on the hill door at Sea House or standing close to the juncture where stone walls yielded to the demand of earth; the sighting of the three beavers, who had perhaps just that day abandoned their dam and gone searching for a new home; Teddy, one arm out, gesturing toward the last floes of ice on the lake; Hale, declaring mystery; Lydia in her hat; and even Iz, like a splinter-faced fire demon wrapped in a cocoon of smoke.

If there were tears, they were hidden by the force of spray; if there was regret, it slid away in the spill of pictures.

Mystery. Something I'm meant to do. Something remaining. Enduring.

———

Cynthia couldn't hear over the force of the main flow and the braided side-rivulets of the stream. If not for its rush, she might have detected Lydia and Hale with Teddy and, a little later, Iz. Two or three neighbors had showed up as well.

"A big rumbling. That's what I heard."

"Andrew was at the museum. I called him and said the beaver dam had given way, and he needed to come. He'll be here any second."

"We've got to find her—could have been swept into the lake."

"Or be pinned by a log."

"Let's each take a portion of the bank."

The voices wavered and fell away without Cynthia ever realizing that others had come near. She had managed to lever the boy closer to the surface of the water without freeing him and now was unsure whether she could lift him into the air.

A woman who lived on the lake road peered over the lip of the bank, saw the white face and hands shining under the water, and shrieked. Cynthia glanced up in time to see her open mouth and the head drawing back.

The running feet and calls back and forth were muffled by the flood...

But Cynthia could not worry about neighbor women. She still couldn't raise the painting, lost her grip and found it again. Some claw-ended debris raked across her hand, though she ignored the smart of cuts. She would have to slide one end up, tilting it carefully to avoid rocks and spars.

"Cynthia!"

She heard Andrew's voice, gone rough and strange, but couldn't look up; she might lose hold.

That crashing noise was also him, tramping along the caved-in bank. She could see from the corner of her eye as his ruined shoes landed with a slap on a jutting stone. He slipped into the water and waded upstream, calling her name.

"Some fool told me you were lying in the creek, drowned."

Now at last she looked at him, though she held the boy in her arms.

A thousand times over, she thought, smiling. *It has happened a thousand times that lovers and mothers and fathers have felt the grief that one was dead and later the upwelling of joy because the news was wrong, dead wrong, and the lost one still as whole as before.*

"No," Cynthia said, "never that."

Andrew grasped the canvas and helped her draw the boy from his grave and steady him so that the painting stood balanced on the rippling skin of the water. Then he reached for her with one hand and kissed her hard on the mouth, the pair of them still holding the canvas upright.

"My sweet Lord!"

Hale was bellowing from the bank, but the two didn't stop kissing. The boy hovered beside them, white and ascendant.

"It must be spring," Lydia cried, peering from the brink. "Get back, everybody," she called. "She's not dead— far from—let's mop out the gatehouse."

They didn't, though, not right away. The neighbors hung their heads over the edge and gawped until they had their fill of news. Even Lydia. Hale declared that he loved the sight of a miracle. Whether he meant the resurrection of the boy or the kiss or the fact that she had escaped destruction or all three in one, Cynthia never found out. When the couple in the stream finally pulled apart, Andrew looked up at the image, its bottom edge supported and pushed by the water.

"Who is he?"

"Don't you know?" Her face glittered with drops of spray. "Just a moment ago it was Ophelia, drowned." *Ophelia. The most terrible thing in the world: what should have been.* Everything could have been different for Hamlet, given a little tinkering early on, but that's not how things played out. And life had come so close to being entirely bleak for Cynthia, as if the girl in her had survived tragedy but withered away with the dried heads of weeds and daisies in chains around her neck.

She felt the joy that had been wakened in the flood of images, bound and twisted with this new thing, Andrew not letting go of her hand.

"But it's not that—"

"Why," he began. He looked at her, puzzled.

"The boy isn't a ghost; he's not your cousin—the one who died in the hill—though I never saw the face near or long enough to get a good likeness. I've made him," she said, "and yet I feel sure he came to make me over to suit himself. You see? He was in the trees by the gatehouse, waiting for me to appear."

"I don't—"

"My muse." Cynthia averted her head so that she couldn't see the boy's face and leaned closer to Andrew. "That's what I think he is. He's not merciful. And is as ruthless as an angel. He's demanding. He doesn't care if I'm cut or lamed or shaking, and he makes me race to keep up. But in the end, he saves me."

Even to Cynthia, the meaning of her words was blurry, as if glimpsed through a dark pane of water.

Andrew lifted her hand and kissed her fingers. Cynthia saw him glance at the ring, saw that he was glad she had put it on.

"You're shivering," he said, "and there's blood on your shirt and clotted in your hair. You'll have to come to us at Sea House. I don't want to lose you to the cold."

———

In autumn, Cynthia Sorrel and Andrew Wild were married in the little church where Father Wren was rector, while a pair of towering glass angels looked down with something like knowledge in their stained eyes. Though the bride's brimmed with tears, not one escaped. It was picturing Teddy, the best man, as a well-dressed beaver in his fine new vest of whitework that kept them from spilling over. Lydia, who was standing next to her and always cried at weddings, kept the tradition and made up for it.

Cynthia's thoughts drifted from the words; she could feel the boy walking among the stones in the churchyard, and a moment later she was sure that if she only turned away from Hale Wren and Andrew and the others, she would see him standing in the back, glimmering naked in the midst of wedding finery. She didn't; it wouldn't do, and she knew the boy was there without looking. The sensation slowly ebbed, and she was made a married woman and blessed and set free to seek the meanings of *love* and *mystery* in the world, with its flood of images and sweet pleasures and work to be done.

The Door in the Hill

Idylls of Glimmerglass

Never has there been a summer like this one, not so long as I can remember," Andrew declared. He slid a hand along Cynthia's arm as she met his bright blue eyes, her heart doing a quick ten-yard dash before he pulled away.

Though it usually rained this time of year, they had had an unbroken swath of fine sunny days, here where the summers often dictated sweaters in July. The one flaw of high humidity meant a pale green that afflicted the air above the lake, smudging Lion Mountain into the sky and softening the hard edges of Kingfisher Tower until it appeared visionary and floating.

They had gone sailing with Teddy and three of Andrew's grandchildren, letting the two boys and girl stand in their water shoes on the submerged island known as Muskrat Castle.

"Funny—why that name?" Cynthia asked.

"Something from a story," Teddy said, waving a hand. He was lying indolently in a deck chair, watching as his brother scrubbed smears of dried sap from the deck. "The usual intrusion of unreality. We're always bumping into bits of romances around the lake."

"We've had more than our share of novelists and poets over the past several centuries. Even if we are a mere village." Andrew looked up but Teddy didn't see. He had closed his eyes and now settled a straw hat over his face.

"Not a *mere* village. The best village," he murmured. "And where else could we live?"

No one answered Teddy's question, as it seemed that no one but Cynthia could possibly imagine another place to live, and she had no wish to argue.

"I'd like to find out how to climb inside the storybook house on Muskrat Hill and look out the invisible windows," Lizzie said. She crouched in the water and made a face at her little brother. "Just think what you might see," she whispered.

Ned let out a howl and staggered toward the boat.

"No, silly!" she shouted. "It might be something wonderful."

"Neddie," Andrew said, "here, grab my hand—"

He hauled the child on board, and Cynthia marveled once more at how one little sprite of seven could be so thin and lively. She could see the veins under Ned's skin and the flick of his heartbeat.

She draped a towel around his shoulders and hugged him close.

"Something tickled my leg," he said.

"Probably a weed."

"Maybe." Narrowing his eyes, he drew back from her embrace. "Or maybe—maybe it was water snakes. Or mermaids. Or water vampires."

Cynthia nodded. "Or maybe it was the lake monster. The very tippy-tippy end of his tail."

Ned made a scrunched face of alarm, half genuine, half mock.

"It'll get Lizzie and Drew!" His words were low and guttural.

There seemed no end to his roles and voices. Just as she hadn't considered that children in one family would be so different, she hadn't known that one child could be so changeable.

"It might," she acknowledged, "but it hasn't gotten anybody yet. And it's old."

"How old?"

"Maybe as old as the hills. The glaciers gouged out the lake and left the little wriggly tadpole behind, and he grew and grew until he was our monster."

Ned perched on her knee, watching Drew and Lizzie climb into the boat.

"You're the best grandmother in the world," he said slowly, not facing her, and she felt a little rush of warmth toward the three, not hers by birthright but as a kind of gift. They were handsome, clever children, and she liked seeing Cooper Patent through their eyes. But only Neddie was still small and wanted to snuggle in her arms.

"Look what I found," Drew called, lurching forward, ducking under the boom. He held out a white clay pipe, the stem broken.

"Isn't that lovely? Some Dutchman must have been visiting Muskrat Castle, centuries ago. And he lost his pipe." Cynthia smiled at the older boy. His face was not as mobile as Ned's. It had a quality of stillness, though the eyes startled with a penetrating stare. Drew was tall and what used to be called *well made*. But he hadn't noticed girls yet. Nor was he half so adept at worming his way into the good graces of adults as Ned or Lizzie.

"Let me see!" Ned fingered the pipe. "It's full of muck."

"I dug it out of the ground."

"Good job. I've never stumbled on one of those." Andrew took the pipe from Ned and examined it before handing the find back to Drew.

"Wash it out carefully," Cynthia told him. "You might find a dottle of very old tobacco at the bottom."

She glanced up as Andrew bent to kiss her.

"Mush!" Neddie thrust at his grandfather's arm, but that just made him kiss Cynthia again.

"Mush, yourself," Andrew said, tweaking the child's ear before he went back to work with a rag and a can of wax.

"I'm going to add the pipe to my collection." Drew had a jumble of broken flow blue pottery and transfer ware that he had amassed from his walks along the lake. He sat down on a coil of rope and began to fish shards from his pocket, spreading them in a fan on the deck.

Drew didn't care for swimming, and only Lizzie had jumped back in the water. As Cynthia glanced over the bow, she saw the slim legs vanishing slowly into Glimmerglass. Lizzie was standing on her head again and, in another instant, she surfaced, blowing water from her nose.

"Did you see that?" she called.

"A perfect headstand. You looked elegant, like the Lady of the Lake withdrawing into the depths. Only I suppose she never showed her legs. Wish I had some flowers to toss you. Something." The painter in Cynthia noted how the girl's limbs glowed in the transparent jade.

Lizzie swept the top of the water away from her in one long green ruffle.

"If I was the Lady of the Lake—"

"Totally beyond the bounds of possibility. She is a mythological being. Or somebody long dead. If I *were* the Lady of the Lake," Teddy corrected from under his hat.

"That's funny!" Ned was abruptly convulsed with laughter. "Great-uncle Teddy can't be a lady! He's supposed to be a bear."

Lizzie dove and swam up once more, her hair sleeked back so that she looked like a cross between a girl and an amphibian, looking about with shining eyes. "Everyone's interrupting me! The Lady of the Lake would throw something at you, wouldn't she? She wouldn't want something thrown to her."

"Well, the sword went back to her in the end." Drew was turning a broken cup in his hands. "Excalibur, I mean. So it got thrown at her."

In response, Lizzie sank out of sight.

"What's the Lady of the Lake?" Neddie whispered in Cynthia's ear.

"From Arthur. King Arthur." Drew had heard him.

"But not Great-uncle Teddy?"

Lizzie had surfaced and was now scrambling over the side. "No, you little idiot. He's no lady!" A rill of high-pitched laughter made Ned clamp hands over his ears. "He's a garden gnome! That's what he is!"

Cynthia leaned forward. "Lizzie—"

Lizzie looked entirely gleeful. "Just look at him! He's got the round tummy and the size and shape and the waistcoat and everything but the little red cap."

"There's a dress-up box with red fezzes at Sea House," Drew told her. "In the blue nursery."

"That's helpful!"

"And that's about enough, Lizzie," Andrew called.

Do not laugh, Cynthia thought. *Do not think about what a curious Humpty Dumpty creature Teddy is, with his dandy waistcoats and his excessive love of pastries and his utter lack of interest in huge realms of experience like any sort of romantic love*

90

or people outside the family or the whole humming world outside Cooper Patent. It's almost as though he is only part of a person living in a tiny corner of the world, and he'll never be quite complete.

Teddy was growling through his hat. Pretty soon he would tug his summer waistcoat into place and sit up to scold Lizzie, no doubt to tell her that not only was she no Lady of the Lake, but that she was no lady at all. *What a scene*, Cynthia thought; *what an idyll, with comic touches*. The girl would laugh at him, her eyelashes dark and spiky, her fair hair soaked. Lizzie was as lovely as a naiad, and she was right—her great-uncle was fit for a garden gnome, especially set next to her youth.

His eyes peeped from above the hat that was now sliding onto his vest, and his brow was wrinkled and looked absurdly wrathful. For an instant, his indignant glance met Cynthia's eyes, and he looked as cruel as a stinging creature out of Faerie Land. *We are not amused, we are not at all amused*, she thought, surprised.

But the cloud of anger slipped from his face, and he was Teddy again.

Laughter tugged at the corners of Cynthia's mouth, so she put her arms around Ned and pulled him toward her, hiding her smile.

The Castle against the World

A year had passed since the wedding, and Cynthia had grown accustomed to metamorphosis. By marriage she had become a wife, a sister, a grandmother, and a mother. This was much to be that she had not been before. Most of the time she liked these new selves and did not regret the loss of solitude. The months flowed leisurely by, and only later did she realize that she had been headed for trouble from the beginning.

It wasn't the outer world, though strangeness had settled over the country. Birds had been falling out of the sky for a year, dying in mid-flight. Yet another war was on, and the bodies of strong young men and women were coming home in bags, to be unwrapped by strangers. At a distance, people were drowning in flood, their houses shoved downhill by earthquakes. A metallic thread of terror shot through the fabric of public life. When she thought about these things, Cynthia felt helpless—as if some creeping shadow of a horror were coming toward them as the sun set. Scandals in the capitals, disease leaping and spreading like a fire arrow that had sailed into dry thatch, a bird's heart bursting in mid-flight: what could she do? She bent over her paper, sketching a child. She held her husband in her arms, resting lightly against him.

In the face of mysterious threats, Cynthia's life seemed to grow more and more dreamy, and occasionally she felt it take on a curious fragility. Even her pleasure in Andrew sometimes seemed insubstantial and wavering—a mirage of shimmering light, soon to be blotted out by the dark. At these moments she might give a little quiver, shrugging off the claims of the outer world. For surely she was happy, harvesting sheaf after sheaf of gold to lay up in some grand post-and-beam barn of memory. Its brightness would chase the glimpses of night away, so that her life felt quite real once again.

She often had the sensation that she and Andrew and Teddy and the others had retreated to this refuge of Cooper Patent the way some wise and dauntless ruler of an earlier age, besieged, might have withdrawn his court to the seclusion of a castellated abbey and taken heart in pleasure and beauty, forgetting the raging tribes and red pestilence of the lands beyond. Yet it wasn't so; the members of the Wild clan were all from the place, or else spent summers there, and she was the only one who had found a new refuge.

Sometimes when Andrew flipped through a sketchbook to see her pictures of the day, when they explored the hills behind the house, or when they cooked together in the big Sea House kitchen—drinking wine and telling stories—Cynthia had a momentary feeling that she had wandered into a fairy tale. Along with this passing sense came the suspicion that she would be made to account for every jot of happiness.

Despite spending many of her afternoons playing with children and sailing on Glimmerglass, she was working well, though nothing had reached the level of the oil painting she had made of the boy in the trees. It had not, in the end, survived its tortuous passage to the pool. Even in decay, the intense green of the vegetation and the pallor of the skin commanded the eye, but the head had been ruined.

Still, she told herself, the hours spent had changed her. The painting was worth the doing, even if the labor ended with its loss.

She considered the idea that she might already have done her best and that such a picture might not come again. It was a kind of failure, she suspected, to entertain such fears. Other times she thought it right, just as needful as considering that there were limits to her time on Earth, and that one day she would cease to be. She had not stopped aspiring to more. Some day, after she caught sight of the boy once again, she would make the picture over. Often

94

when she saw the canvas propped in her studio, she felt a pure pang of grief because she could no longer remember his face.

The painting she had done of Teddy now hung in what traditionally had been called the *third-best parlor* at Sea House. Oddly, there was not one named *second-best* or *best*. One day she and Lydia were having tea in the room—they were all addicted to the lazy ritual of afternoon tea, Lydia and Hale and the brothers and Cynthia—and her friend scrutinized the image, cup in hand, sipping as she looked.

"Isn't that peculiar?" she said softly.

"Isn't what peculiar?" Cynthia crossed the room and peered over Lydia's shoulder.

"Something. Something that I'd never noticed before." The teacup clinked onto the saucer.

Cynthia waited. Lydia was a close observer of her pictures.

"There's a subtle slyness to the face. I hadn't realized it before," she mused.

"Perhaps it's an error of sight—perhaps I didn't read him right."

"No," Lydia said with decision. "He looks like himself. I just didn't see properly before. It's as though he had a secret."

"My fault," Cynthia said. *It must be. Who could be more genial and less sly than Teddy?* "Perhaps I made a mistake to have him sit at that angle. A sidelong glance can look shifty."

"Maybe," Lydia said.

And that had been the whole of the conversation. They moved swiftly to other topics, as if something faintly disgraceful had been mentioned that did neither of them any credit.

The exchange came back to her later, and more than once she paused to look at the portrait. Often in the past she had felt that a picture revealed more than the artist knew. Of course, it was possible to be faulty in execution. An element in the face, somewhere about the eyes, bothered her—not just the slantwise stare but also a certain crimped quality to the lids. She thought of redoing the painting. Yet she could not quite decide about the sitter. Surely any suggestion of slyness was due to a failure of skill, or to an intermittently seen impishness in his face, she concluded. Something of the asexual, mischievous Puck seemed to color Teddy.

Because her brother-in-law had been her guide to Sea House, it seemed ungrateful to even consider Lydia's words. While Andrew was at the museum, Teddy had frequently tempted her away from work and taken her on strolls through rooms at a distance from the portion of the house that they regularly inhabited. She loved finding herself on the threshold of some mysterious chamber shrouded in ghostly sheeting. And he had a way of flinging off the dust cloths that aroused expectation. If the room turned out to be charming, the two of them might sit and read there, or fetch a tray of tea. After a few days of getting to know the spot, she would help him cover up the furniture again, for Sea House was far too much for three people to manage. She was fond of these peculiar picnics

96

and felt that her brother-in-law must be a kindred spirit to have conceived of them in the first place.

Cynthia often glimpsed the housekeeper, Mrs. Tabitha Griffin or "Bitha," in the distance, dragging a vacuum, a feather duster under her arm. Now and then they exchanged pleasantries. Once she encountered the woman in an unfamiliar corridor and asked her about the work.

"It's a good enough living," she told Cynthia. "No need to go scouring about for new houses to clean. Always something to do. One room after another and all the same to me. Furniture and drapes to dust, cobwebs to clean. No interference from the bachelors—no offense! I'm just that used to it being the two. But let me know if there's anything particular you want done."

"No, no, there's nothing—"

"See, there's peace to working here because you know the job's not going away. It's just like that family of Amish boys—you seen them yet? They come by once a year to repair a section of the roof. That roof seems to go on forever. Steady work is what it is."

Bitha gave a severe nod and walked off. It was the longest speech that Cynthia had ever heard her make. She supposed the housekeeper was letting her know how she liked things to be. *No offense but no interference.*

"Pssst!"

She looked around. Who else was in the house? She often had an uneasy sense that she was not alone, or that someone might be spying on her.

"Oh, you! You scared me!" She laughed at herself—why had she jumped?

"Come see what I've found." Teddy leaned from an open doorway, waving at her to hurry. As she came closer, she glimpsed the two moons of his glasses, obliterating his eyes. He only wore them for close work.

"Andrew still out?"

"He won't be home until 4:00."

"Too bad. Well, he'll miss the fun." He gestured toward the interior.

Cynthia paused on the sill. A gold-flowered pitcher and washbasin stood on an ebony stand near a bed hung with green brocade that matched the walls, sheathed in cloth. A dusty wall hanging depicting a topiary maze had been dropped on the floor. At the opposite end of the room bulked an enormous wardrobe in black veneer with engraved bronze and pewter inlay. The effect was startling, the dark, frilled pieces of French Baroque crammed into the narrow chamber.

"What's this?"

"Come in, come in!" Teddy seemed all suppressed excitement and agitation, his forehead gleaming with sweat in the lamplight.

"It's awfully grand for a bedroom." She stepped inside.

"The room—our cousin, Theophilus Moss Wild—my Aunt Penelope's son. The doorway was hidden behind that tapestry, but I don't know why I couldn't find it before, since I've looked often enough. This monstrosity of a family home is too much for anybody to compass."

"Who are—"

"The one who died. Inside the—you know where—the hill. We called him *Moss* because *Theophilus* was a mouthful. His mother used to call him *Theo*. I can just hear her voice. 'Theo, darling Theo,' she'd say. But I don't think any of the rest of us were darlings . . . just her children. I was also a *Theo* back then. After he died, nobody called me *Theo* anymore. They went back to babyish *Teddy*. And that was that."

"She must have been dreadfully unhappy when he disappeared." Cynthia thought about Drew, sweet and thoughtful, and merry Ned. She touched Teddy's hand in sympathy. He grasped at her fingers without appearing to pay attention to what he was doing, squeezing them hard until she wanted to pull away.

"Oh, she was, she was. My pretty Aunt Penelope. They all had long names in that branch of the family. A name wasn't worth anything if it didn't have four or five syllables." He dropped her hand and began to search through the wardrobe.

"Penelope Wild. It's a pretty name."

"We could hear her crying, all over the house. You couldn't get away from the sound. And that's strange because often I couldn't hear a noise in the next room. But that weeping! It was so fierce. Her tears seemed to saturate the air. Impossible to get away from the cloud. We all felt oppressed by it, accused and unhappy, though she didn't mean to make us feel so." Teddy was fumbling with the knob on a square door in the wardrobe—a cupboard for hats, Cynthia thought. "I adored her. In the idiocy of boyhood, I somehow thought that I could replace Moss.

That she would set me in his place and be comforted. But I couldn't. Not at all. I still feel rather bitter about it, I'm afraid."

"No, I don't suppose that would work. Did she have other children, or was he an only?"

"Oh, there were more. Bartholomew, the one we called *Goose*. Why, I don't know. Elizabeth. She was *Bideth* to the grown-ups and *Bug* to the cousins. Ariadne. *Ree*, we called her." Teddy turned away from the door for an instant, looking bereft. "She was mad about her children, my lovely Aunt Penelope. That's the sort of person a loss comes to, so often, isn't it? Fate is annoyed."

"Maybe those are just the mothers who remember and talk about their sons and daughters, so that we know they've suffered. Maybe others remember but keep quiet. Couldn't that be it?"

Cynthia was surprised to see that her brother-in-law had tears in his eyes—so long ago, and he still felt a pang. It touched her, made her feel the tenderness of the man and think that she had wronged him in talking with Lydia. The flaw was surely in the eye of the painter.

"Not my aunt. She kept herself quiet all right; she killed herself, not long afterward. She'd told Andrew's mother that she couldn't live, knowing that a child of hers was lost, not even his body recovered, not even a grave to visit. But Aunt Philippa just told her that she had to give over grieving and remember her surviving children. Philippa could be very firm. She wanted people to buck up and do their duty. She said that the other son and her daughters needed her—and that all the cousins loved her and were trying to make things right." Teddy's hand trembled on the knob, and he rattled the panel and tried to force it open. "Penelope was our favorite. Each of us probably thought that we'd be the one to console her. But nobody could."

"How terrible!"

"Yes. Yes it was." He tied a handkerchief around the knob and began wrenching at the door. "Very shocking. There was even some nonsensical muttering about burying the body at a crossroads in the old-fashioned way, but in the end they dug a hole and planted her in the churchyard. Her doctor sang in the choir, and he intervened. Afterward, the rector of that era declared that my dear Aunt Penelope had been out of her mind with sorrow and hadn't known what she was about. Only I think she knew very well."

"That's so sad. What did you mean about the room—was this hers?" Cynthia felt that it was too claustrophobic, with its narrow dimensions and hulking, elaborate furniture, for a married woman's intimate chamber.

"No. Moss stayed here when he was visiting. They lived a few miles off in the country, but he often slept over. His sisters were the first Wild children to go away and not come back to live. We lost them. The death somehow spoiled things for us all. We were as thick as Ali Baba's thieves until Moss died. Six or seven of us were fairly close in age, too." He stared off, his eyes winking behind the glasses. "If I'd only known what would happen...."

The latch gave way under his fingers, and he swung open the door.

"Ah. Here's something." Teddy picked up a tiny wooden box, opening it to display a velvet liner. "Just before my cousin died, an uncle gave him a ring that had belonged to our great-grandfather. Moss's birthday was the week before. Seventeenth birthday. And I believe this case held the ring. Our family always put a lot of store in such gifts. Things handed down, jewelry and pocket watches and so on." He reached in the cupboard. "Here's a journal. And a picture."

Cynthia took the photograph from him. The black-and-white checkerboard frame was at odds with the rest of the room. The boy in the studio portrait had tied his hair back in a ponytail and wore a loose paisley scarf at his throat instead of a tie.

"He has an intriguing face," she said slowly, "oddly handsome." The eyes were deep set under dark eyebrows. Irregular features reminded her faintly of Andrew's cragginess.

"It's hard to remember. Was he interesting? I don't know. It seems to me that he was, but I can't think why. I suppose because he was our cousin."

"What did he like to do?"

Teddy shrugged. "They all played the piano in that branch of the family, and they sailed and fished and hiked and rode. Moss was intelligent—quick at math and fond of blowing up things in the woods behind the house. He always had a chemistry set. I can't think why my aunt favored him, although she had intimations about people. My Aunt Bess said that Penelope knew Moss was in some kind of danger before anybody realized we cousins had

102

gone into the hill. Said she knew things about the death that hurt her to madness. Doesn't that sound dramatic? Bess was always the drama queen of the family." He took the picture from her, studied it briefly, and set it down on the bed. "Andrew says that Moss built a small water-powered turbine and generator at boarding school, but I don't know about that. I knew him, but now it seems so long ago."

Cynthia flipped open the journal and read aloud:

> *Theo says we should take food and candles and a ball of twine so we can spend the day poking about the tunnels. I don't know. Andrew was angry because the hill is uncanny, and he told me that the whole idea is a fool's game, that we shouldn't go without telling our parents. I rather like the idea of finding out everything that's beyond the door…*

"Was it your idea, Teddy? *Theo's* idea?"

"To explore the tunnels without an uncle along? Maybe. I don't recall. Andrew sounds remarkably well behaved there, but he wasn't, not really. Probably he was as eager to go inside the hill as we were. I don't really like to think about it, so I don't, mostly." He was rummaging in the drawers below the hat cupboard. Swollen with humidity, they came free in a succession of jerks. "I ought to soap them," he said, shoving one home.

"I feel chilly, just imagining it—going into the dark and never coming home again. Being buried alive. That must be the most frightening way to die." Cynthia picked up the picture once more. The boy had lovely eyelashes.

103

And there was a small red birthmark in the shape of a droplet close to his hairline. Had his mother feared it when he was born? Was it prophetic of blood and tears?

"Oh, I don't know," Teddy murmured. "Death is an ingenious fellow. There's bound to be worse."

"I'm lost, you know. I didn't come here on purpose," she told the picture. "And would like to go back to the front parlor and get away from you. Poor boy, you make me sad."

"At Sea House, we're always lost." Teddy was down on his knees, rooting in the lowest drawer. Somebody had left a torn pincushion in the back, with a scrap of cloth attached by a still-threaded needle. Fine sand leaked slowly through his fingers. She saw that he had burst a button on his Lincoln green waistcoat with the pattern of worsted keys. He must have been very eager to search the room.

"Still, I can put you on the path back," he said, "if you like. Go thataway." He signaled with the pincushion, strewing silt. "Take the third door on your left. Go past four rooms and take a right, and keep going straight until you see something you recognize. That might work."

"Third door," she repeated.

"So long as the rooms stay where they're supposed to be."

"I'll have to blame the rooms," she said, "when I get lost." She lingered, curious as to what he was doing.

He had managed to remove the drawer and now began feeling at the back of the wardrobe. "I'd help you, but I want to see—Moss was a great one for secret hiding places."

"Before he found the very last one," Cynthia said, her hand on the doorframe.

"What?"

Startled, Teddy gaped at his sister-in-law. Once again the moony reflections blotted out his eyes.

"The one nobody could find," she said.

———

It seemed to Cynthia that Teddy was bent on exploring every cranny of Sea House, despite his claim that nobody could master the place. Often he would appear almost magically before her when she rambled about the mansion. He would guide her to some remote curio cabinet, its shelves jammed with carefully labeled specimens of birds' eggs, tropical butterflies, or crystals, each numbered in India ink. Other times he proved as capable of getting lost as she was.

Once he had stepped out of a secret compartment in the wall, his hair netted in cobwebs.

"Puck," she had whispered, seeing a touch of the sprite in his grin.

He had swept the tatty weavings away with his fingertips and bowed.

It appeared to her, too, that Teddy possessed secret radar and knew whenever she was drawn to the hill. One summer's day, she leaned against the paneled wood and listened to the voice of the sea inside, feeling a cave-like coolness against her skin. Tiny beads of sweat that had

105

gathered on the face of the door moistened her arm and cheekbone.

"Tempting, isn't it?"

She whirled around, heart thudding, but it was only Teddy.

"If the key hadn't been lost, we could open the door to our own little underworld. It's always chilly inside. The air would feel good on a hot day, wouldn't it? Perfectly safe. There's a knob on the other side."

She pulled away, her sleeve sticking to the wood.

"What happened to the key?"

"Nobody knows. I was just looking for it again. And Andrew won't let us bring in a locksmith from out of town to make another. I'd like to, but it's his house, not mine." His voice didn't suggest even the faintest trace of bitterness. "The hill was locked after Moss vanished—after our uncles and men from the village made a series of searches and couldn't find him. That's the only time we've had policemen in the place."

"They couldn't find him." She wondered what that meant. How big was the labyrinth behind the door? Perhaps it was not orderly but more of a maze, confusing and doubling in on itself.

"No."

"Do you remember what the inside of the hill was like?"

"Not really. It was a long time ago. We were lucky to get out again." Teddy brushed his hands together as if to remove a layer of filth. "Funny how dust in old houses makes your hands feel as though you can't get clean. Like grave dirt. I had the idea that the key might be hidden in my cousin's room. Silly of me, I suppose. I thought someone might have put it with his things. But there's no sign of one, and now I've looked through all the rooms where the cousins stayed. No key."

"Why is it, I wonder—why should anything be in there? Inside the hill, I mean."

"My great-grandfather told my father that our ancestors scooped out hiding places because of the Cherry Valley Massacre. But another time he said that it had been there from the start, part cave and part dug-out passages."

Teddy took a small box from his pocket. When it creaked open, he peered inside as if expecting to find an answer.

"The housekeeper from when I was little—Bitha's grandmother—always told the children that the hill had been used as a quarry, once upon a time, and the original cottage had been built against the opening to catch the coolness in the summer and the heat in winter. She said that the Indians and wandering whites mined here before anybody thought to build a house."

Cynthia's mind still dwelt on the dead boy. Was Teddy holding his ring box? Had he taken it from Moss's room? She wanted to see the faded color photograph of the boy again but didn't want to ask. The loose scarf like a cravat, the wide lapels of the jacket: she remembered these perfectly. Long eyelashes. Eyes, lodged somewhere between blue and green. The thin nose, slightly irregular. A teardrop like blood. She had a good memory for details. Yet how to put them together? Like an image seen once in a kaleidoscope, the face had fallen apart in memory.

"I'll see you, Teddy," she said. "I need to go paint some more."

It was strange how glimpsed boys had taken hold of her imagination, ever since she had moved to Cooper Patent. She thought that she might try to sketch Moss from that one brief look at the photograph. It wouldn't be accurate—no more right than an oil painting of a boy seen twice, never up close. She looked at Teddy without seeing him and passed on down the hall.

"He was a gimp," Teddy called after her.

"What do you mean?" She stopped, and a pier glass in the hall seized and held the wavering reflection with its surprised O of a mouth until she turned to stare at him.

"His leg. One was shorter than the other."

Cynthia was trying to bring the boy into focus. A handsome kid, son of the lovely Penelope. Face a little irregular. The Wild relatives tended to be good-looking, with long limbs and thick hair and blue eyes. Teddy was the only one she had met who didn't fit that mold. *The garden gnome.* Yet in his way, he was appealing. And Iz. She had forgotten about Iz. *I've been neglectful*, Cynthia thought; pleased with her new life with Andrew, she always failed to remember Iz.

So she sketched for the rest of the afternoon and then stopped by to see Iz with a basket of flowers and fruit. And was glad to go home again afterward, to feel the faint, invisible fire that poured from her skin when she ran to meet Andrew at the door. When she kissed him on the mouth, she remembered Moss, blowing up things—old toys? cast-off pots and baskets?—behind his home. Perhaps traces of explosions were left on the grounds here as well.

Now and then in the days afterward, she imagined Moss at school or play, tinkering endlessly, loving experiment and change. She thought about his delight when electrons began leaping from atom to atom, spilling over with energy. Sometimes when she pictured Moss, she saw him as radiant, combusting, motes of him pouring into the darkness behind the hill.

———

That summer she often passed by the mysterious door, for no good reason.

She never thought to go to the spot when Andrew was at home, but when he was absent, she felt a faint magnetic pull. Neither she nor Teddy ever spoke of the entrance in front of Andrew, and over time it became like a Bluebeard's secret between them—seldom did she linger for more than a few moments without her brother-in-law coming across her there. She believed that he must sense the same loadstone force that drew her. But she didn't feel it when Andrew was at home because he had a magnetism of his own.

Blessed with copious energy, he always wanted to be doing. She had sketched him cooking, planting trees, repairing a chair—a hundred busy activities. Bent over the Sea House bills with papers and envelopes tossed in a drift at his feet, he still managed to appear alert and quick.

Once when he was at the museum, she knelt and stared through the keyhole of the door into the hill, one hand pressed over her heart. She could see not the smallest splinter of sunshine.

"That's life."

Spooked by her own shrill note of surprise, she jerked upright. And there was Teddy, lounging against a lacquered chest-on-chest, his vest a smolder of brocade fire in the shadows.

"You frightened me." She spoke in reproach, but he only laughed.

"Always a shadowy door. A hill and mysteries lie behind every house and family."

"I suppose we make our own darkness. If that's what you mean." Cynthia rose, startled again at hearing a distant halloo. "What's that?"

"It's Andrew. He's home early. Somehow I didn't think you would want him to find you here." Teddy gave her a mischievous smile. "I'm surprised he hasn't walled up the maze by now."

She stared at him, feeling vaguely uncomfortable.

"I don't have any secrets from my husband," she said slowly. "How could I?"

"Well, then. That's all right, isn't it?"

"Yes," she said, "it is." The familiar glad eagerness came to her, and she forgot Teddy and hurried to find Andrew. She could hear a voice calling her name; she wanted to fit his body against hers and to touch the shock of hair and kiss his lips.

There! He was sliding an umbrella into the Chinese stand.

"Andrew!" She hurled herself at him, and he laughed, rocking her from side to side.

"Let's go; I want to get in an hour on the water." He bent and kissed her neck. "Just us, out in the middle of the lake where nobody can see."

For a moment, she couldn't speak, caught up by his desire—feeling as though they were joined at hip and breast.

But the words of her brother-in-law had planted a seed, and she did, in time, come to fear that there was something like a secret between them—shared with Teddy and standing like a door between two lovers who had meant to let nothing at all divide them. The suspicion disturbed her. She made a resolution to stay away from the hill, and she kept it for a long time.

Her Fine Resolve

In August she found the key.

She and Neddie had been clambering up the slope behind the house, looking for fossils among the outcroppings. The little boy's pockets bulged with finds, some revealing an intaglio or a relief of ancient, long-dead forms, and others disclosing their special mysteries only to his inward eye.

"Here." Cynthia held out a snub thing—a gray clamshell perhaps, stuck to an equally gray rock. It was about as pretty as a bunker poking up from a field of churned-up mud.

"That's a good one. Thanks." He forced the fossil into a pocket. Neddie had six pockets, two behind and four in front. How long would the shorts stay up? Already they were dragging, showing the jutting bones of his hips. Earlier he had complained that they were too big, but Cynthia doubted it.

"We're getting up high," he said with satisfaction. "Grandpa and Great-uncle Teddy look this little." He held his forefinger and thumb close together, taking the measure of the tiny figures. "Pinch!" he shouted. "Gotcha!"

"There was entirely too much relish in that grandpa-squashing," Cynthia said. She bent over, inspecting the ground.

"I got Teddy too. Squashed him like a Japanese beetle."

"And what've you got against Japanese beetles?" She handed him another rock, and he shoved it into a pocket with barely a glance.

"I like them. They look all dark and oily and shiny. You know those rainbow puddles you see by the road, where the cars drip?"

"Uh-huh."

"It's not cars. That's really where the beetles do something. Maybe where they're born. Or maybe it's Japanese beetle poop. From their beetle *bobmims*." His head rocked back as he let out a maniacal laugh.

"What do you mean, *bobmims*? You're awfully silly sometimes."

This sent him into a paroxysm of crazy laughter.

113

"Stop that, young Ned!" Andrew called up from the front lawn. He was tinkering again, head and shoulders under the hood of his Jaguar.

"Fooh." Ned was instantly quiet, eyes sparkling as he watched his grandfather shift his weight, leaning against the car.

"E's got no 'aid!" the little boy exclaimed.

"I can see that I missed a great deal by not having an older brother or an older sister to lead me into the realms of the ridiculous," Cynthia told him, dropping a crystal into his shirt pocket.

He fished it out again and inspected the fingerling of quartz.

"Jewels," he muttered, "precious jewels. More, I need more—what's that?"

"What's what?"

Neddie squatted, staring at the crest of the hill.

"I saw somebody. Up in the trees. Watching us." He surged to his feet and took off running.

"Wait—"

But he didn't. He was going full tilt at the slope and, built low to the ground, he was making good time. Cynthia followed, calling after him. Once, twice, three times: a glimmer of whiteness caught her eye.

She was panting, occasionally pausing to catch her breath but afraid to lose sight of Ned. Loose stones slid underfoot, but she kept pushing upward, her gaze on his skinny legs. At the summit, he stopped to look around and she caught up with him, grabbing his wrist.

"He's gone."

"Who?"

"I don't know. He wanted us to come, but then he went away." Neddie sat on his heels and began combing the ground. "I never come up so high," he confided. "It's nice here."

"Nice?" Cynthia was still out of breath. "Ha." She searched slowly along the curve of the hill but saw nothing.

"I did see him," Ned murmured.

"Sometimes I see things, too."

The rocky soil on the steep slope abruptly gave way to grasses, low plants, and a grove of spindly trees. Cynthia wandered along the border that divided the green world from a stony one, nudging the occasional moss-bound fragment with her toe until it broke loose. But she found no more fossils this way.

The sheen of metal caught her eye, and she bent to pick it up. But the prize was gripped fast by plants and mosses. Working it back and forth, tearing at roots, she fished up a tarnished key.

"What is it?" Ned trotted over to look.

"Nothing, Neddie, just an old key." Funny how children had a second sense for other people's discoveries.

"Maybe to a treasure chest."

"Maybe." But Cynthia knew what she had found.

"Can I have it?"

"No," she said, giving him a hug. "This one's mine."

"Wah." He squatted and began to pick the dried dirt from a fossil.

She saw something else and knelt to pull apart a tangle of low-growing plants. It was a crack about a foot long. She slipped her hand into the gap. Then she pried up a pebble and dropped it inside the hill. From the sound, she guessed that the stone had slid a ways before ricocheting off rock and at last falling into silence. Tempted, she slid the key into the slit as if into a gigantic keyhole.

"No! What are you doing?" Ned was jigging with anxiety. "You can't throw away a treasure key. You can't!"

But she could, couldn't she? And if it vanished, there would be no more temptation to search for a lost key or to open what perhaps should not be opened. Barring a locksmith, the door in the hill would be a dead end.

The key would slide along the shaft, clinking as it collided with obstructions, sailing into the sound of the sea. Perhaps she would hear a distant strike of metal against the floor of the cavern.

She looked up at Neddie, her fingers barely gripping the shaft.

If she did not let it fall, the key could disclose the mystery in the house once more. It was all before her like a task in a fairy tale: the cleaning, the polishing until it was burnished silver, and the decision. She half resented the demands of the blackened thing. Life wasn't a fairy story, though; she wouldn't be drawn irresistibly through a forbidden door, only to find bloody bones and girls' shifts strewn around a Bluebeard's well. She had married no wolf of the forest.

She withdrew the key from the opening.

"Don't tell anybody, okay? I'll clean it up and keep it in case we find a treasure chest. Our secret, just you and me."

Neddie whooped and then wheeled in a victory dance, leaping, stamping the earth, striking at the air with his hands.

She watched him, spellbound, until he flopped onto the ground in mock exhaustion. A second later, his head popped up. He snatched up a nub of quartz and turned it over in his hands with an air of great excitement. What an actor he was! Every move seemed fluid, as if he were aware that someone could be watching.

No, she didn't have to toss the key. She could choose.

A Coupling

She waited all of a week.

Day by day, Cynthia thought about unlocking the dark. Sometimes she considered that her first impulse was right: the best way would have been to let temptation skitter into blackness. Perhaps the only correct act was to signal defeat. One couldn't master mystery and might as well yield the key to destruction. Other times she felt that the lightless, breathing stuff behind the door was waiting for her to admit the sun from Sea House into its depths.

By the seventh day she had made a decision.

She wanted to delay until Teddy was out of the house, but he was seldom gone. The Moon Gate shop muddled along without him most of the time, though he often called the manager to talk. His buying trips were infrequent. He appeared to have adopted a steward's role at Sea House: a proprietary function like the post of warden at Father Hale's church. Perhaps he resembled one of those fossilized ocean creatures in the stonework, a snip of slow life fettered to a magnificent, lustrous shell. Perhaps he was a squat vestal virgin, bound to the flame on the home hearth. However it was, Cynthia had observed that he often seemed uneasy and out of place elsewhere. So she slipped quietly to the door in the hill when Teddy went to his room for a nap; Andrew was at the museum for a Saturday afternoon meeting. She felt a touch guilty, remembering how her husband had kissed her passionately and said that he wanted to get home to her right away.

She judged that the key weighed about as much as an old coin-silver serving spoon; it was symmetrical and brushed with fine scratches. Only the asymmetrical teeth took away from the harmony of a cast metal head made from two simple spirals and a graceful tapering toward the shaft. Cynthia had shrouded the key in a handkerchief, just in case she encountered Bitha, who claimed that objects such as keys belonged to her domain. She put her hand against the door, fearing both the silence and the flecks of sound that marred the silence—even the sea-like pulse of blood in her own ears.

She would just see if it fit.

The key bobbled at the lock until she held it steady with both hands and slid the teeth into the hole. She felt the shaft slide forward and catch. Yes! It was the right one. She pressed lightly at the key. The teeth had engaged in the cylinder. With one hard rotation, the door would be unlocked.

Carefully she removed the key and swathed its brightness in Andrew's handkerchief.

"That's enough," she whispered, "just to know is enough."

Her heart was still flittering fast. Hearing something that might have been a footfall, she swung around to search the corridor. A shadow slid along a distant wall, and a spark of sun blazed at a window.

No, nothing.

Her fingers ached. She had been squeezing the nape of the key.

"I'm a grown woman," she told the empty hall. "I can do as I like."

But she suspected that it was not true. Who could do only what she liked without regret? Grown, though, she was grown, at least if she relied on her birth certificate. But every time she stretched a canvas, she knew that she was still a lonely child trying to catch at the world, beginning with the blank expanse again and again and again.

She shoved the key into her pants pocket and fled through an open doorway. The room inside was pretty, with damask curtains and a marble mantelpiece and a Chippendale chest-on-chest lording it over the lesser furniture. She hardly saw the pictures anymore, though once she had been struck by their charm: the far wall was hung with silhouette portraits of the family. The jet-black profiles with their coils of hair and curls and stiff eyelashes held still and watched her pass.

The Fatal Door

The key now rested in a jewelry chest that had belonged to her grandmother. Cynthia pushed home the top drawer and stood staring, her fingertips on its smooth bird's-eye maple. A flicker of movement in the mirror before her woke her attention.

"Andrew!"

She whirled about, but it was only Teddy.

"Sorry—I didn't mean to startle. What have you been up to?"

Cynthia could still feel the curve of the metal against her palm.

"Nothing much. Just working on a commission, trying not to give in to a cold and sore throat. Plus a bit of sightseeing around the house while you were napping." Had he seen her slide shut the drawer? She didn't want to share the key. Not yet.

Teddy was fussing with his waistcoat, tugging at a thread. The burgundy waistcoat, Cynthia noted. Small cerulean birds navigated his equator and marked out the rungs of latitude.

"I was just getting out my ring." She lifted her hand to make sure he could see the emerald, flanked by pearls. "Didn't want to ruin the pearls with turpentine and paint."

She would tell him sometime. But not now. Because it wasn't pressing, not really—though he would think so, Cynthia suspected—and at this very moment all she cared about was finding her way to Andrew, who was calling her name. He would be leaving in the morning, attending a pair of meetings, the first in Aspen, the other in San Francisco. Teddy had laughed at him because the meetings were about museum outreach to under-served communities. "You'll be lounging in a Jacuzzi, with candles flickering on grotto walls and aspens shivering close by, and you'll be chatting about bringing art to the poor! How ridiculous! Why not stay home?"

Andrew didn't want the trip now, at least not without Cynthia. But he had promised to accompany the president of the museum when the arrangements had been made more than a year before.

"Come on, Teddy! Let's hurry—we'll go pick rasp-berries for dessert and have a picnic."

His face brightened; he loved eating out-of-doors. "There's your leftover onion tart and tapenade. We can have a salad and bread and a bottle of wine. I'll whip some cream for the berries. That would make a very respectable picnic."

"Yes, fine," she called over her shoulder.

She meant to mention the key to Andrew, but as she didn't want to tell in front of Teddy, she didn't bring it up at dinner. The three of them ate at a table under the grape arbor, musky and dark with fruit, and the meal was so pleasant that she entirely forgot the door to the hill. The key came to mind later on, as she lay on the bed, sipping a glass of wine, and watched her husband pack his suitcase. The moment was wrong, she decided.

They went to sleep early, and when she woke in the morning, Cynthia was running a slight temperature. By the time a car came to fetch Andrew for the drive to the airport, she was glad to be staying home.

She went to the front door in her bathrobe, standing just behind Teddy. "Don't kiss me," she said, "just in case." But Andrew kissed her thoroughly anyway, boasting that he never got sick.

"So I suppose you won't go anywhere if you're not feeling well," he said.

"Maybe this is just a passing fancy," she said. "If I go visiting, I'll call your hotel when I arrive. Leave a message on your cell phone. Or something. I might scoot down to the city and collect some supplies and go to galleries and a show at the Met."

"If you don't want to put it off until I'm back. We could go together."

"Yes." Her voice was muffled against his chest.

"Are you two just ignoring me?" Teddy was smiling, but he looked petulant. Cynthia guessed that he wasn't used to sharing good-byes.

"You take good care of her." Andrew winked at Teddy. "I knew you were there, but you're hardly worth the kissing."

"Huh." His half-brother cocked his head as if to display his cheek for a kiss.

Andrew laughed and detached himself gently from his wife. "Russell hates to be kept waiting. I'll bring you a surprise."

"At your second stop, I wouldn't mind a Chinese parasol, the kind with wooden ribs and oiled paper," she said. "If you see them. Otherwise, just yourself. That's all I really want."

"What about me?" Teddy stamped his foot, looking so much like an indignant Tweedledee out of *Alice in Wonderland* that Cynthia burst into laughter, though she wasn't quite sure whether he was teasing or was, indeed, ruffled.

"What does anybody ever bring you but a vest?"

After wheeling his suitcase to the car and hoisting it into the trunk, Andrew hurried back for a last kiss from his wife.

"Teddy, make sure she takes care of herself, okay?"

"I thought Russell hated to wait," Cynthia said, clinging to him.

"Tough for him."

A minute later, Andrew was climbing into the back seat and then waving until the car swept out of sight. Cynthia felt let down. She shivered, wondering if she was well enough to sketch. Perhaps she would sit up in bed and draw the contents of her room, or the scene outside the windows.

"Teddy, could you stand to ask Bitha if she would bring me a mug of tea? And maybe a piece of shortbread from the canister."

He shrugged. "I suppose so. I've got to fix myself breakfast, so I'll tell her. Do you mind if I park your car on the road above Izzie's place?"

"Why?"

"I was thinking of having a group of friends over, and there's not quite enough parking."

Cynthia didn't feel like going anywhere. If she did, later on, she could always send Teddy for the car. So she fished the keys from her bag.

"Don't lose them," she said. "That's my only set. The others went overboard when Andrew and I were sailing last week. And please don't forget to ask Bitha for that cup of tea."

Instead, he did it himself, fetching a tray with a mug of tea and a piece of shortbread. A bronze monkey hugged the handle of a bell beside the plate.

"You can ring if you want me. I told Bitha that she could have the week off." Teddy perched on the edge of the bed. "Should I call her back? You don't look so good."

Cynthia was surprised, as Andrew always joked that if they didn't have a few hours of daily wiping and mopping from Bitha, the house would fill and become an enormous dust bunny. And once or twice she had speculated that Teddy's real love and care was saved for the mysteries of Sea House. By extension, that included Andrew, who had inherited the place.

"If you don't mind fetching tea now and then," she said. "I'm not feeling all that wonderful."

He patted the coverlet where it lapped her feet. "Sure. I'll take good care of you." He got up and wandered around the room, pausing by the jewelry chest to examine a cameo that she had left on the dresser top, his close scrutiny reflected in a Georgian wall mirror. And then, finally, he trickled out the door. Cynthia was just as glad. She felt feverish, and her throat hurt.

When Andrew called from Colorado, she claimed to be "feeling fine, just a little under the weather." She didn't want him to worry. It was only a week until he would be home, and by then she would be well. The ache that had settled in her muscles would pass. She dozed for a while, and when she woke, it was already dark.

She rang the bell, but Teddy didn't come for a long time. He eventually brought a cup of soup and a cracker and fetched a winter throw because she was trembling with cold. Afterward, he vanished and did not return.

"He doesn't want to be sick like you," Cynthia told her reflection. The image in the giltwood frame nodded but looked pale, with two hectic spots of fever on her cheeks. After eating a few spoonfuls of soup, Cynthia left the tray outside the door and took a hot shower. Still cold, she dug out a winter gown to wear over silk long johns.

In the mirror, she looked like a stranger, the garnet wool throw cocooned around her. In only a few minutes, she was asleep.

When she woke, the sun was molten at the windows, and the blaze hurt her eyes. A sharp-edged pain had sheathed itself in her chest. She felt hungry, but Teddy didn't come when she rang the bell.

"Men," she said.

After combing her tangled hair, she cloaked herself in robe and throw and ventured to the kitchen. She couldn't detect any sign of her brother-in-law and wondered if he had parked Andrew's car out of sight. Teddy was, she remembered, expecting company. More likely, he had driven it to town to buy supplies, as he didn't have a car of his own. She drank some tea for warmth and swallowed a few pills, but nothing much in the way of food appealed to her. Finding a packet of biscotti in the cupboard, she slipped it into the pocket of her robe for later.

How seldom she was alone in the house!

The old place stirred like a ship straining against the wind.

"Teddy," she called out once, sure that she'd heard a snatch of music. "Funny to have an old home like this without a ghost." A faint echo of the words unnerved her, even as she felt sleepiness drenching her limbs.

She put her head down and dozed for a few minutes, waking with a jerk. The key had appeared in her dream, floating in the darkness. She had been about to take and slide the shaft into a keyhole of night.

"I could," she whispered.

She got up and checked the hall—nothing—and glanced out of a window overlooking the front lawn. Despite the sunshine, rain dripped from the eaves and the grass and trees were hung with jewels. She asked the air, "Teddy, where are you?" Still no sign of a car near the house.

Passing his room on the way to her own, she knocked but no one answered.

"Strange."

He must be gone, though it was unlike him. She hoped that her wandering brother-in-law would think to bring her some juice and cough drops.

The shut door made her remember the dream of the key.

Cynthia swayed and then closed her eyes. Surely she could take the key and unlock the door, let it swing open. She felt too sick for more than that, her curiosity like a flame half smothered by ash.

Fumbling at the wall, she paused to rest. In a few days she would be better, she told herself, and she could draw and paint again. But now she would cool her hot face, and after that she would go to her room and sleep until Teddy returned.

She was drifting, lost in a fog…then she was back in her room and her fingers were on the chest, and the drawer opened to disclose the silver key. It was such a long walk to the door in the hill! Yet she found herself abruptly there, as if in the peculiar manner of dream travel. Waves of low fever pulsed and made her recall that whatever was inside breathed with a sound like the sea. The wood felt icy to her hand, and she dropped the key twice before it slid home and the teeth engaged. The bolt flew back. At her tug, the massive door inched forward with a clang and a groan. As it swung toward her, cobwebs were dragged across the Oriental rug by the threshold.

She leaned on the doorframe and stared. The inside was jet black. Only slowly did she see anything beyond the sill. Dust lay thick over a crimson runner, and she made out a table, gray with fur, against a chiseled wall. On the ground close to the door was a bundle of church tapers—heavy wax candles fit for an altar—next to a box of kitchen matches, both sealed in cellophane: evidence of the boys, or perhaps of those who had searched for the missing Moss, long ago. Perhaps the supplies had been left to help any who might need them.

Coolness poured against her face, and she was glad for the wool throw around her shoulders. When a flush of warmth made her tremble, the photograph of the dead boy flew into her mind, as if conjured by that dreamy heat.

"Moss." The word made a small, shivery echo. She felt grief for him, and closed her eyes as a single feverish tear streaked her face. The mound behind Sea House was an immense catacomb with only one occupant.

Her eyes flashed open, straining against the darkness. Whirling, she stared at the hall, its shadowy recesses seeming to glow next to the pitch inside the hill. She had imagined quick running steps over carpet, the twitch of a floorboard underfoot.

Nothing. Not even a shadow stirred.

"Just three steps."

She would leave after that, and another day she would tell Teddy and Andrew what she had found and how she had tried the key in the lock. A fear that her husband might be angry swept over her.

The ground was not level but pitted and uncertain to her feet. She glanced back to see that the hall was empty, though made subtly different from before by the three steps she had taken. Ahead, a black nothing seemed a speaking silence. A tinge of dread brought alertness, and she felt as if she might soon discern what the gloom had to say.

Then all before and behind her was blotted out by a mighty slam.

A scream had flown from her throat and was battered into echoes against the stone. She heard a click of metal. When her fingers grazed the knob, cobwebs came away in her hand. Tugging at the door, Cynthia found it immovable, though she could hardly remember—was the key still in the door? She knelt and peered through the glowing keyhole.

"Teddy!" she shouted, but there was no one in sight.

Surely she must have left the key in the lock. She searched her pockets but found nothing but the biscotti. Yes, she was positive now. But there was no key—only the chink of light. If a wind had blown the door shut, might the concussion have knocked the key to the floor? Yet the tide of air had been flooding from the hill into the house, not the other way round.

"Oh." A blink of dark interrupted the constant brightness of the keyhole. "Teddy! Teddy! Is that you?"

Though she yelled until her voice grew hoarse, no one answered. Fever washed over her face and seized her body with cold. She sobbed briefly but was restrained by the sheer unreality of what had happened, though some moments of panic made her beat on the panels until the door thundered and her knuckles bled. Once a whine sang from her mouth and vanished. She couldn't get her mind around the shape of what had taken place.

Would she stay trapped inside the hill, to die and leave her bones with those of the missing boy, Moss? The thought came to her but drifted away. As the minutes passed, she could fathom less and less how the door had come to be closed, or even whether things were as they seemed—was she, in fact, suffering some delusion of a fever dream? Her head ached when she tried to remember what had happened. Groping, she found the package of candles and clutched at them. But a wave of weariness swamped her. She lay down on the floor, the throw like a caul around her body, and fell asleep.

The Labyrinth at Sea House

Lady of Pain

Near the door Cynthia had picked up fistfuls of Hansel-pebbles, white as drops shed from the moon. Now they were almost gone, though she still had matches and candles tied up in her makeshift shawl. The biscotti had already vanished, the last crumbs in the package shaken into her mouth. Her knuckles were bruised and flecked with blood. Perhaps she had been delirious; although usually adept at picturing space, she couldn't map and hold this shadowy region in her mind.

She had gotten used to the rough walls—had ceased feeling the tomb shutting around her. At a low moment, she had howled for Andrew, willing the sound to reach him, however far away. He would follow her voice like a thread across the world, she was sure of it!

But certainty fell away, and she walked on, holding a candle.

At some point, impossible to plot, she noticed a change. It must have come on slowly, while she moved in a walking sleep.

Sewing needles were strewn on the walkway. She caught sight of one, two, and then a sprinkle of six or seven, glowing faintly in the dark. Soon her low-heeled slippers made a crunching on the metal, and the radiance underfoot increased. Some were fine quills such as quilters use, but others were larger, some big enough to load with packthread, some with eyes wide enough to bear a fine rope.

The path of needles glimmered ahead, ducking into corridors, reappearing as a distant shine. It resembled a yarn like mohair, oddly soft and fuzzy in the dark, dipping and emerging as if sewn.

While twisting through a tight elbow of passageway, she glimpsed a figure, and only the rawness of her throat kept her from crying out.

She hurried over the uneven floor, the package of tapers banging against her hip. Who was the mist-like walker, deep in the night of the hill? Not even a moan of fear—unexpected, startling, her own—could stop her from pursuit. The candle's flame guttered and was swept away, but she could see by the uncanny foxfire of the needles.

Trembling and soaked, she at last was only a few feet behind the slight form. *A woman, it was a woman.* Fine luminous splinters pattered onto the floor; ahead was gloom.

Cynthia caught up, staring in fascination at the needles piercing the woman's skin.

"Iz." Her voice was a croak.

But Iz shook her head impatiently and did not respond.

"It's me."

No recognition showed in the woman's face, nothing but blankness.

"Andrew's wife," Cynthia said.

Iz frowned at her. "How did you get here?"

"I—the door shut behind me. It must have been—I was alone, Iz, and had the key—"

A bright needle emerged from the iris of Iz's left eye and sprang to the stone.

"Don't call me by that name. I don't know you." Iz lit a cigarette and blew smoke in her face.

Coughing, Cynthia waved away the cloud.

"My throat hurts so," she whispered. "What should I call you?"

Iz tapped at the cigarette with her forefinger, dropping ash onto the needles.

"Call me Our Lady of Scars, Our Lady of Needles, Our Lady of Pain—call me whatever you like, but not that name,

Iz." Her mouth was crimped in anger as a burst of needles shot from her cheekbone. "Open your mouth."

Like a child, Cynthia responded obediently, sticking out her tongue.

"Needles," Iz said, "nothing but sharps and quills." She cupped her hand at Cynthia's neck.

The soreness grew abruptly worse and then stopped. Cynthia stared at the burr of needles resting on the woman's palm, some of them embedded deep in the flesh.

"Feel better?" The voice was sardonic.

She felt deeply confused. "Where are we?"

"The Sea House labyrinth, of course. Don't mind me; I'm not altogether here." A short, mirthless outcropping of laughter made a barrier between them.

"But why? Why has this—"

"You are a bit helpless, aren't you? At least Andrew wasn't fool enough to marry a girl of twenty. I suppose you do something interesting—"

"A painter." Cynthia clutched at the candle, terribly anxious. "I lived in the gatehouse, and we fell in love."

"And you don't know why you're here."

"No, I don't. I want to go home—"

"A gust slammed the door shut. Is that how you lied to yourself? There's no wind deep in Sea House. You'd have to raise every window to lift a breeze. Don't tell me you didn't see anything, didn't hear—"

"Maybe a shadow, a click—"

"Who would lock you in the hill?"

"Not Andrew," she whispered. So much had been burned up in fires of fever, she didn't remember that he had gone away.

"No," Iz agreed, "not Andrew. Though I like to blame one or the other of the cousins for my troubles. Usually Teddy, as he's such a fool."

She grimaced, showing a flash of teeth. "He's the one that sent Iz out in the rain, the night she crashed his sweet little car. Does he have another yet? Or does he just borrow Andrew's? Poor old Iz. They had to pick the spikes and pins of glass out of her face." When she swung her head, hundred of needles flew from her hair, some striking Cynthia in the arm and sticking in her gown. "He was fond of that car, but she's dead and gone now. Like Iz. Half of her, anyway. The half that lives in the labyrinth with the Wild ghosts."

The path now resembled a forest floor quilled in silver pine needles. Little eyes and big eyes winked around them: the ground was watching, and it made Cynthia feel dizzy.

"What a stupid, sickly thing you are." Iz sucked on her cigarette and let the smoke curl from her nostrils.

"Iz." She drew the little name out pleadingly.

"Don't use that name again." Iz stubbed her cigarette against the wall and let it drop. "I see you," she added. "You're an idiot, aren't you? Andrew's wife, another fool, who could have a thousand eyes and still not see. You know nothing, you see nothing"—here she lit another cigarette—"this is a world of needles. Shut up and you might hear the sound of it shifting under your feet."

Cynthia stared at the needles clinging to Iz's hair. The harvest just fallen had already been replaced.

She felt desperately thirsty; when she reached into her pocket, searching for help, her fingers closed on a Hansel-pebble. Slipping the tiny white stone in her mouth, she sucked at its smoothness.

"Why—"

"Why?" Iz turned the cigarette in her fingers, shaking her hand free of a shower of silver. "Why is the world so wretched? Why is it a world of needles? Why did Iz go out that night when she'd been drinking?" Her voice slurred, laced with venom. "Or try this: why does he hate you so?"

"Who?"

"Who do you think? What could have happened, and why?" She made a little mewling noise. "You're a fool, blinkered as a bat without radar."

"You couldn't possibly know—"

"Why did he love his aunt too much and want to keep her for himself—why did Moss Wild never come home? Why was he glad when his unfortunate sister-in-law, Marian, died of lupus? Why did Theodore Wild lock Andrew's pretty new wife in the Sea House labyrinth?"

"No." Cynthia's voice was as small and faltering as a cricket's chirp at the tail end of fall.

"Yes, oh, yes. I, Half-Iz, am a seer. With my little eyes, I spy that Teddy would hate, hate, hate for Andrew to take another wife. Andrew is his half-brother, his companion, his altogether. Poor old Teddy Bear, stuffed with rags of hate. You never saw some sign?" She barked a laugh.

140

"What's left of Iz probably hates you too, out there in the world. She hates them, doesn't she?"

Half-Iz. Cynthia let her eyelids fall, remembering the shadow, the sound of a footfall, the click. "I don't believe you," she said. Her tongue found and pressed the pebble against the inside of her cheek. When she opened her eyes again, Half-Iz was blowing smoke rings, one through another.

"Who are you?"

Half-Iz kicked at the needles, and they swept upward in a surf of dangerous light. "Our Lady of Pain, didn't I say so? And you are a fool. Me, I'm just a ghost out of the past. She died, you know, Iz did. She really did. The glass needles pierced her face. She was broken on the wheel. Can you imagine somebody wanting to hold Iz's heart in his hand—massaging it to life? That's nearer than any lover. She went to hell, Iz did, and she dragged back a piece of its fire. That's Iz, the grating old bitch. I'm just her demon fingerprint, or the shade cast by her anger. I'm a half-ghost. I have a hundred names and no name. This place—it has a meaning to the Wilds. It goes back a long way with them. If there are Wild spirits, this is where they haunt the living."

Iz-shadow, Cynthia thought. *That's what you are.*

"How do I get out?"

"Get out? Simple. It's impossible! So you do the impossible. You lived at the gatehouse, you say—then go through the gate!" Iz-shadow's voice jeered at her: "Go through or die."

Cynthia sat on the floor, worn out by talking. She lay down on the glowing needles, drawing up her legs and swathing her head in cloth. Iz-shadow was scolding, laughing, but Cynthia ignored her.

Fever lapped over her head like a shawl made of sea. Even as she slept, rocked on the tide, she could feel the needles stirring under her body and pain like slow drops bringing hurt and wisdom. In her dreams, she was more like one dazed from a blow than a sleeper.

The Needle's Eye

When Cynthia woke, Iz-shadow was perched on a tall rock, legs crossed, reading a paper. The wreath of smoke around her head made her look like a demon.

"You're awake," she said, and nodded. "Welcome to woe."

Without answering, Cynthia watched her pore through the newspaper. Although the rawness in her throat was gone, she still felt weak and hot, her limbs and head aching. She heard the far sound of a bell, as lonely as a buoy. The Sea House maze was phosphorescent with needles piled on the floor and clustered in bunches on the walls like spiny urchins. She could hear their metal striking the newspaper and sliding.

"What's the news?" she whispered.

"The daily rot. Some tormented girl, a boy vanished behind the door, deaths by misadventure, general brokenness, and suicides botched. Car wrecks, with glass to be picked out of a woman's body."

"But where does the newspaper come from?" She rolled onto her side, tightening the throw around her shoulders.

Iz-shadow ignored her. With a cigarette, she lit the flimsy paper. After much fire-edged smoldering, it went up in a sheet of flame before dropping in flakes onto the floor.

"I hate them—hate all the secrecy. They smile and speak double, all the harassers—"

"Who?" Cynthia had gotten onto her feet while the newspaper was burning. Now she reached as if to touch Iz-shadow on the arm, where a long ropey scar was bleeding silver.

"Get away! Don't—"

Iz-shadow kicked with sharp-toed boots, catching her on the elbow.

"Ow! You have"—she groped for a word—"substance."

"Idiot," Iz-shadow said, her voice without rancor. "You thought, did you? That was a mistake. I'm all substance of hatred. I'm hate of sophistry and Babel and careless talk and deception."

"But why hurt me?"

"Why not?"

"And why did you—why did Iz cut—those scars along her arms?"

Iz-shadow shook her head. "Trying to get somewhere else, maybe? Somewhere very quiet. Yet she left the half-ghost that's me here. Perhaps I came when she died for a few minutes, before they picked the glass from her body? It wasn't safety glass, either: nothing safe about it. Iz flew away, right out the car and through an old storefront, into a maelstrom of splintered glass."

A grin exposed her small, sharp, heavily stained teeth. Lighting another cigarette, she dragged on it, slowly vanishing into a cloud. A voice came out of it.

"Who'd want to be Iz? Here, at least, the needles are visible. That's clarity. I couldn't bear to be like her, hating most everything yet also loving some of what she hates— weird and twisted. Andrew. Teddy. They're nothing to me, but to Iz! What agonies." Smoke further obscured her perch and dimmed the light radiating from the needles.

"I didn't know. But she's wrong about so many things." Cynthia waved a hand, dispersing the acridness creeping into her eyes and throat.

The shadow was silent, and when she went nearer, fanning the smoke apart, Cynthia found that the figure was gone. The needles shifted under her feet, shining with undiminished strength now that the haze had dissolved. But no light led into the distance: nothing. Had the substance of Iz-shadow been taken into the cloud? Her own fingers had been innocently combing the smoke apart, rending it into streamers and nothingness. It seemed possible because at

145

this instant her own flesh felt trembling and insubstantial, as if it could waver and spring into dust with a puff of breath.

Near the spot where she had lain down to sleep, there were needles of gigantic size. She put her fingers through the eye of one of these and felt an intense cold that made her withdraw the hand in haste. Others, even larger, lay off the path. She knelt and peered through an eye and saw nothing but motionless cloud. Through another she glimpsed a lake, the color of burned azurite, with white limbs and faces faintly visible through the waves. Something played along the surface: a vapor, or perhaps flame, of clear, unscorched blue. One eye was a porthole onto a scene of ships jockeying, their masts piled high with snapping and billowing sail upon sail, thrusting toward a harbor where pennants were flying. A gold and silver tree blossomed on the shore, holding up immense cups like magnolia blossoms. The smell of an unknown perfume wafted against her face.

As she drew nearer for a better look, she tripped on the trailing garnet throw and plunged headlong through another eye.

The Opal Bone & the Minotaur

On waking, the first thing she remembered was the faint *ping*! of metal against stone. When she found a needle, Cynthia fastened it through the cloth of her nightgown. It pricked now and then as she walked, and the hurt seemed to make her not more wakeful but sleepier and sleepier. Whether it was the effect of what had happened to her inside the hill, or whether it was because of fever that flashed along her spine and sent messages of heat and chill toward heels and fingertips, she moved slowly and looked about with only a drowsy curiosity. The ground underfoot was velvety with moss; the walls of the Sea House maze had utterly vanished. She still walked in a labyrinth—high topiary laid out in corridors that led gently downward. At least, that was the direction she was going, perhaps merely because *down* was more pleasant than *up*. The shrubbery hadn't been trimmed in a while; what looked like wild landscapes of sprigs and tiny trees crowned the top, and Cynthia thought dreamily that if only she could scale the leaves, she might find herself in another realm entirely and walk, insect-sized, under the airy sprouts.

Because the idea of marking a trail had left her long ago, she was content to drift, taking whatever opening was the nearer. Now and then she followed a crook of the path to a dead end, where a slim flowering sapling invariably marked the stop, its branches thrown up a gesture of seeming helplessness, as if to say, "I don't know—couldn't possibly—only that this is not, not the road to—wherever." Sometimes she cast herself onto a soft green mound and looked up through frothy spring branches at the sky.

"I fell. I fell asleep. I could sleep for a hundred years."

The words hung in the air and only slowly dissipated.

Later on she reached meadow-like passages. Flowers bloomed and knotted into seeds; the young trees that marked dead ends turned to gold and plum and persimmon. Snowflakes slid into the long grass and lit on the throw, their traceries glowing against garnet. The labyrinth abruptly released her at a lake's edge.

Though snow barely dusted the surface, the lake was quite frozen and easily bore her weight. The ice seemed at least a foot thick and shimmered with blue, green, and rose.

Despite daylight and common sense, the low sky that hugged the scene appeared as if lit by an aurora borealis.

Padding farther onto the lake, she searched the shores for signs of habitation, but only evergreens were visible, with an occasional topknot of branches punctuating the walls.

"Can't rest here."

Still gripped by sleepiness, she wanted only to lie down on the ice and doze. Feeling a faint panic at the idea, she pricked herself with the needle in an effort to wake up. The lake looked stranger than ever, a maze-bound sheet lacking the sprinkle of icehouses and fishermen with pocket flasks that meant winter at home.

A figure was slicing slantwise across her field of vision. If she hurried straight ahead, she might intercept him and could ask for—well, she would think of something.

At first her feet moved sluggishly, but as the cool air pressed against her face, she felt more awake and began to run. She could decipher the shape better now. Someone was carrying a parasol and toting a burden on his back.

She let out a cry, hoping to slow him, but he ignored her, skating steadily on. The pain in her chest had returned, and chills rippled over her arms.

"Wait, wait—"

Still calling, she dashed after him. At last he swung around and halted, watching as she slowed.

"Please—"

The saliva in her mouth tasted of metal. She paused, shivering and unsure, a hand lifted to shadow her eyes from the pale, diffuse light of the scene.

"You look familiar," she said. "How can that be?"

"Why not something you would recognize?" He folded the fluted parasol with a snap of wood slats and oiled paper, tucking it into a drawstring bag.

Certainty came to her in a rush as her glance fell on the hands, veined with white fire, although where she had glimpsed him lay just beyond her grasp.

"Where have I seen you?"

He examined her face. "Between Fair and River, perhaps?"

"Fair and River? The streets, you mean?" The memory of Cooper Patent came back to her, and with a pang she remembered Andrew.

"Father Hale Wren, the church... Do you recall?" His mouth was a sober rose, and though the eyes were blue, their whites gave them a fearsome strangeness, as if a candle shone from behind.

"That's not possible!"

But she had seen him standing near the door; she knew now. The smears of snowy flame in the robe, the necklace like leaves cut from verdant ice, the otherworldly flesh like breathing opals: when the sun intensified, the image would flare into glory.

"What are you?" She was helpless to ask more.

"What could I possibly be? I might be a butterfly, a hummingbird, a cataract, a cicada, a dragonfly, an angel, a branch of lightning—there, that narrows things down a bit, doesn't it?" Amused, he cocked his head to one side and inspected her. "And you would have a name, I suppose."

"Cynthia." She stared at the mass that she had assumed to be a burden, but at closer sight proved wings of a pale amethyst.

"Ah, yes, one of the old moon goddesses. No wonder you can walk on water." He was teasing, she was almost sure.

"And you? You are—"

A rainbow pulsed through clothes and skin. "Some call me *the Angel of the Cuttlefish*. Between River and Fair they call me *the other Tiffany angel*—my colleague being the angel with the broken face on the far side of the sanctuary. Some say that one is no Tiffany at all. It doesn't matter. But you may call me *the Opal Bone—Bone* if you must have less than that."

"Why not *Opal*?" She shook her head slightly as if to clear it of a mist of unreality.

"Why would I wish to be called a thing that a man would be called?"

Cynthia looked at him. *Why indeed?* "But men aren't called *Opal*—oh, you meant a human. If you're an angel, is this Heaven?"

The wings stirred, releasing the resinous fragrance of burned myrrh.

"This? It's set up to be man-made. A fellow came and started digging and planted twigs. After a while he gave up and lay smoking a clay pipe under the basswood—there was only one tree back then—and started to dream. And he discovered what everybody here discovers eventually, that he could dream something into being. Out of homesickness, I suppose, he named it *Glimmerglass—*"

151

"I see! It's our own lake, only changed."

Bone seemed a little tetchy over the interruption, his feathers ruffling and tongue making clicks of reproof. He started walking away, not asking her to follow, though she did, keeping a short distance to one side.

"It's quite different from the lake near Fair and River. The resemblance is only illusion." The angel searched the ice and then gestured. "See there? That's like nothing anyone had seen around here—massive logs with the bark not stripped off and that big projecting roof. But passers-by think the camp picturesque, and so it stays. Perhaps he was distracted because sometimes it looks one way, sometimes another."

"A Muskrat Castle where somebody could live was only in a story," Cynthia said.

"It's nothing to me." When the angel shrugged, a feather slipped to the ice. "Though I knew about him once. Between Fair and River. I used to walk there before the windows came and even before the church was raised. Lots of dreamers between Fair and River, one century or another."

Bone pointed downward. "Right here the man dreamed up some birds—have you seen them? I really like the loons. They sound eerie and tremulous, as if they're afraid of the dusk coming down. He must have been terribly homesick for the loons because they came out sharper than almost anything."

Cynthia had snatched up the feather and now thrust it in the pocket of her robe.

152

"I didn't hear anything at all like that on our lake—no loons—what happened to him?"

"Perhaps he found another lake. A healing lake of fire to burn away his troubles, maybe—some people like that sort of thing."

Breathless, Cynthia wanted to grasp at a sleeve and hinder his quick steps, but she couldn't bring herself to do so. The robe seemed to be as alive as the angel and likewise veined with scintillant white.

"Look!" She dropped to the ice, rubbing flakes of snow from its surface.

To her surprise, he glided back to where she knelt.

"Oh, yes. He did that, too. Busy man. I sometimes suspect that he was not quite normal, if you take my meaning. Imagine choosing to practice water burial here and then making the ice so clear over the spot. He failed to dream up the living, so he chose to dream up the dead. But a corpse is always a disgusting object."

"Water burial," she murmured. Currents had swept the grit from their faces. One was a mature woman with dark floating hair, one a robust-looking young man, and the last was a pale girl—perhaps not as vivid and striking as the other two but attaining a purity in death that Cynthia found moving.

"I suppose he did it because he felt buried here," Bone continued. "Like you."

"I'm not buried!"

"It seemed so to me. The man was looking for something down in this world. Then he went back and—"

"And what?"

Bone shrugged. "Told stories, I suppose. You see? He was like you."

"But I don't tell stories," Cynthia said slowly.

"No? I took you for a mythmaker. They're not so common where you come from."

Cynthia stood staring at the ice. Why was she here? It seemed that she had known once. But now she was not sure of the reason.

The angel was arrowing away from her on stony white feet. She gave the fictional dead a final glance and chased after him. He seemed purposeful, as if recalled to a task.

"Wait," she called to him, the breath knifing in and out of her throat. She gasped, pressing a hand where it hurt. "So where are we really?"

He spoke with force, without turning toward her. "In an infinite maze whose center is everywhere and whose edge is nowhere."

"What does that mean?"

He gave a dismissive wave of the hand. "It's hard to explain—we're on the outskirts of something you would call—"

"What?"

"Hush. Hear that sound? I can't stay here. I have enemies—"

"What do you mean?" Cynthia whirled around, scanning the shoreline.

"Angels are at war. We've been so for thousands of years."

"You can't leave! How do I get out?" Here she tried to clasp the angel, but he easily evaded her arms.

He had grown taller, as if the opaline flesh had been gaining strength and substance from the ice.

"Far off, demons seethe in the air. Like the shuddering of leaves before they fly from the trees in fall." Bone seemed to take on vigor from his outsized, operatic claim. His eyes flashed, the whites of them brilliant and the blue irises going sapphire. Again she had the impression that a pale fire burned inside his skull. "Even men can feel something evil pass by."

He took the bag from his shoulder and fished out the Chinese parasol. He opened and shut it with a dissatisfied air and then slid it back into the sack before rooting in the depths once more.

"I'm surprised you didn't feel anything before he slammed the door."

Cynthia was taken aback. "What do you mean, he? Do you mean at Sea House?"

"I caught a fragment of something—not so far from Fair and River."

"Teddy—Iz-shadow said—was it Teddy who closed the door?"

"Not my errand to solve the puzzles of humankind. But perhaps what happened will be of use to you. I suspect," he mused, "and think, yes. Of some good use. Perhaps. This is your work, after all. People who come here are looking hard for something. And now, good-bye, worldling." His features displayed a statue-like calm, and Cynthia's brittle self-restraint smashed against it.

"I don't even know how I got here," she cried.

155

"This spot in particular? Most people fall in," the angel said. "One misstep and there you are. A fortunate fall, don't you think?—or not—someone pushed you, I should imagine, over a parapet. That's the way it usually happens with my kind. One minute, paradise—the next, you're a dropping star, pointed to by small human children."

"How do I get out?" Her voice swooped upward, as if she hoped to break through his glassy surface with a single high note of panic.

"Get out? Out of here?" Bone's stare was like the beam of a lighthouse, catching her full in the face. Then he looked off, and when he spoke, his tone was unconcerned. "Die, that's one way. Of course, there are others."

"What others? How?"

"You tumbled through the eyes, I suppose? Perhaps you can do the same, or near enough." The angel reached in his bag once more. After much groping, he withdrew something glinting from it. Without a word, he stooped and forced the thing into the ice.

It immediately sprouted sharp silvery horns. Cynthia squatted, watching as a stem coiled downward, dividing and branching into antlers, thickening into a bole.

"Beautiful," she whispered. Beside her, the tormented shapes of roots jabbed at the air, making knifelike arcs. Past ice, she could discern metallic buds that broke to release lunar blossoms.

"So beautiful." For an instant, everything seemed to be complete and to make sense, but then she lost the thread again.

156

"I hadn't noticed," the angel said, "but I see it now. Humans care for such things. Beautiful and not-beautiful and so on."

"But you're the Tiffany angel by the door—how could you not know what's beautiful?" The window's brightness fell like a star through her mind.

Questions floated up, but she had no time to ask, for the angel stiffened and became as flat as a sheet of glass. For an instant, the gloomy effulgence of the skies gathered and poured through his robes and skin, casting their colors onto the shimmering floor of Glimmerglass.

"Tell me how—"

The angel plunged sideways through the ice like a blade of light. Cynthia patted the surface where he had vanished, but it was already sealed as though nothing had passed that way.

"Wait! You said the man—you said everyone here can dream things into being," she shouted. "Did I dream you?" She listened but heard nothing from the ice, only the wind in the trees and her own words echoing: *dream you, dream you.*

She wanted to follow, to demand answers from him.

Through the eyes, he had said.

She bent, peering through the frozen lake. A blurred figure stood upside down from where she knelt. When she touched the silvery bark of the tree, the ice around it seemed to yield to her fingers. Gripping the trunk, she pressed downward until her arm and shoulder were caught.

She let out a frightened cry. Flying fish or birds were skipping through the frozen lake. Taking a gulp of breath, she shoved her face into the ice; halfway, she began to run out of air and rammed her forehead through to the other side. A little farther and one eye was caught below—one above—the surface. She might as well have been pinned in a cleft of rock, for strength now failed her. Pain, redoubled, pierced her chest as she saw the angel stride away. On the other side, he had no wings, and she saw the draperies flutter and reveal his dazzling shoulder blades. He walked in a rage of brightness that robbed her of the last vestiges of movement, so that she lay helpless while specks of black floating before her eyes joined and blotted out his glory.

One panicked push freed mouth and hand from ice. Slowly she hauled herself along by branches—right side up, as it now began to seem, gravity casting its mantle on her. The angel was gone. Blood seeped between her fingers where she had cut herself on a twig. The flowers were closing, pulling themselves inward to knots of seeds, the beginning of fruit.

"Glimmerglass."

She sat on a thin metallic limb for a time, wondering if she now knew the place. The sky was as heavy and dark as stone—the color of the little finger of Kingfisher Tower that reared its admonition in the distance.

Something like a wish flickered, firefly-small, inside her.

Slipping down, she began to explore the lake. When it hurt to breathe, she pressed her palm hard against her breastbone. Where Muskrat Castle should have been, she saw a stronghold made of blocks of ice, though she didn't stop—she had seen something moving in the distance and hoped it might be Bone. Why hadn't she thought to ask him for healing? But perhaps angels didn't do such things, particularly angels who watched the world's vacillation without pity between River and Fair. Occasionally she seemed to be sleepwalking and dreamed that she was hunting for something lost. It was always something as vivid as stained glass—an emerald bird, a fiery red setter, or a glowing white horse.

Catching sight of a figure in the trees, she veered onto the path of a frozen stream. She had stumbled not into a wood but into stone. The passageways grew irregular and cramped. Shadows and cries and the sound of running feet didn't make her afraid. She was not bothered by hunger, or by the flames of fever that played around her body. Somehow she had become used to them and accepted the fire as an element of her very being. But she was tired and thought without letup of finding some safe place to sleep. The walls were a relentless stone without windows, intermittently open to the sky.

Through gaps, Cynthia saw a bit of whiteness once, twice, three times. What it reminded her of remained a mystery. She leaned against a rock, arms and legs tremulous, and searched her pockets for a crumb—something sweet that would still the shaking. Nothing. Could she eat wax? What had she done with the candles? She must have set them somewhere and then forgotten…. She lay down on a floor that was unmistakably ice. When she pushed with her palm, it didn't give.

Nauseous, she spat up a spoonful of mud-colored grains.

Cheek against cold, she lay shuddering for a long time, drifting in and out of a dream.

She woke to find a dark, muscular thigh close to her face and moved nearer to its warmth. Fingers, tipped with long nails, combed through her hair. Turning slightly, she saw a face with horns that curled upward from a projecting brow. The eyes looked at her with a pitying expression.

"Poor child," the minotaur said, patting her on the shoulder.

She was breathless and couldn't speak. It seemed that she had expected him all along; the way was, after all, a labyrinth.

"Relax. Best not to fight." He took out a bronze emery board and began filing. "Cuticle," he explained. "It causes me no end of aggravation."

Afterward, he removed a small lidded pot and a square of chamois from a skin bag at his waist. The smell of the ointment caught in her throat. He dipped the cloth and rubbed at his horns.

Noticing her once more, he attempted to be consoling.

"Yes, it's this way for so many. They float along in a dream of merriment and distraction, and suddenly there's me."

The words rolled over her, round musical syllables hot against her skin. Cynthia could see the delicate rose-silk lining inside his nostrils as he bent to look into her eyes. The high polish on the black horns made them gleam like the hood of a newly painted car.

160

She still couldn't speak, though the thoughts tried to spill from her mouth in words. *You're supposed to be a guide. Like Bone. Aren't you? You're supposed to help me.*

The air was suffused with light, and she remembered the lake and forest by the gatehouse. A wren flashed across her vision and was gone.

I was looking for the boy in the trees.

I wanted to catch images like fish from Glimmerglass. And in turn they would glimmer and flee and I, I would run after them. I would be quick and light-footed.

That's what I'm doing here. That's why I came.

I just didn't know it.

And I don't want to lose why I'm here again. I won't. In every labyrinth there must be a thread. I won't lose my thread.

Brightness made her eyes water, and she closed them. She heard the air panting from the tunnel of her throat, louder and louder like the sound behind the door at Sea House. It frightened her, made her heart jump and scramble to get away. Her arms and her legs were still quivering. Cynthia concluded that she must have been startled—that would be it; how good to know why she had felt so ill! Fear gradually ebbed, got lost in the back-and-forth saw of breath. After a while, she relaxed at last with a lovely, floating feeling.

When her eyes flew open, she could see the ice floor, the stone, and the minotaur. Although dangerously close to the sharp horns, she wasn't worried, and it was only little by little that she understood that the body slumped beside him was her own.

Moss

Like a skein of silk threads, she was tumbled along the ceiling by the least breeze. Sometimes she washed back and forth as if caught in the shallows of a wave. In her rolling, she lost sight of the minotaur and the body; she forgot everything but confusion. If she had been able to think clearly, the spirit girl might have thought that decades had passed while she was idling in the vault of a roof. When a puff of wind blew her into a low-ceilinged corridor, she was glad of the stillness and the dim light. During this lull she heard someone chanting as he wandered the halls.

He sang a half-familiar story about a hearth where a little fish became a glimmering girl with apple blossoms in her hair. The foam of flowers, the shiny scales of a fish, the sensation of running barefoot in the moonlight all came to Cynthia then, and these were the first things that she remembered.

Later, a line about silver apples made her recall the moon with the prick of a star like a stem to one side. Memories of the old life came sliding back to her— something read about in a storybook a lifetime away. The shape of her was that of a girl about seventeen years old and wearing a white dress and garnet shawl, with a needle tucked into the fabric near the shoulder.

"Hello."

It was a pleasant voice, she considered, and went on staring at the ceiling. An enormous cricket hung upside down and waved his antennae only an inch from her airy nose. When a current nudged her, she keeled over, an ephemeral arm dangling.

"You need somebody to lend you," the voice went on, "a little gravity."

Someone tugged the fingers on her left hand. When her head flopped to one side, she eyed him. For what seemed years, everything had looked vaguely familiar—one ceiling being so much like another—and the sensation did not die away as she gazed at him. He looked up, a boy about her own age, his hair pulled into a ponytail. His eyes were a lovely sea color, deep set with long eyelashes.

"It took me years to get ballast," he told her. "Let me lend you some." With a sudden jerk, she was sledding through the air and growing heavier until her feet slapped onto the pavement.

"Oh!"

"It helps," he said, "with the floatiness and mist. The mind wanders off if we're not tethered."

When she reeled, the boy put his arms out to keep her from diving to the floor. She leaned heavily against him. *The floor wants to see me fall*, she thought, peering into his eyes.

Although she had once been a rather serious girl, she found herself light-hearted and wanted to scamper off. But she had to learn how to walk again.

He was patient, steering her around corners and over ruts in the floor. She quickly became fond of staring at him and learned the shape of his irregular nose and the almost invisible cleft in the chin by heart.

"Come on," he said, once she regained the use of her legs. "I've never liked this place."

Taking her hand, he hurried her away, not hesitating at turnings and passing through deserted rooms without a glance. Ice over pavement turned to ice over earth and then water, and soon they were rushing over a lake that appeared frozen beyond melting—as if winter had lasted for centuries.

"We'll take the stairs."

A stairwell drove into the lake at a steep angle, its aquamarine perishing in a lower story of emerald. At the bottom, the boy hesitated, looking at her uncertainly, and stepped into the ice, drawing her after him. This time she was not afraid and did not find it difficult to pass through the solidified lake. In a moment they were flying along, hand in hand.

Coming to a door, the boy ushered her inside.

"This is the Glimmerglass ballroom. The floor's wonderfully slippery."

Cynthia found herself whirling about the floor to music from a wind-up Victrola. She hardly took her eyes from the boy's; he was smiling, a few strands of his hair fluttering free from the knot at his nape. On their third circuit of the room, she noticed that the fluted horn was a huge morning glory blossom with a pearly throat, the sort commonly sold as *heavenly blue*.

"What's your name?" Something was coming back to her. Names were what you found out when you met someone. And she was…she was searching.

"Call me *Moss*," he said.

She leaned her cheek against his shoulder, pondering, but could not make sense of him: *who was he*? She felt sure he was important.

"Were we something to each other, a long time ago?"

He laughed and didn't answer except to pull her close—nearer until she passed through him as neatly as she had passed through ice. She felt a burst of joyfulness as she slipped through his beating heart.

"I was looking for something," Cynthia said. "Maybe it was you."

"You're taking on ballast," Moss said. "Mind-weight. That's good."

"That's good," she echoed.

Reaching into his pocket, Moss produced a button. "I want to give you something. Hold that. It'll do if there's nothing else."

She examined the button, gold with a stamping of griffins. It conjured the merest atom of memory. *Griffins on a gate...* She didn't have time to go there, to remember. She pushed the image away.

Instead, she recalled her mother's button box. She remembered playing as though the buttons were alive, putting them into families by color or shape, feeling the faint clink of life as she moved them together or apart. The griffin button tingled on her palm as if it, too, might be a living thing.

"Looking for something," she said again. "I wanted to make something alive. I was hunting for something to make."

"Found it—here, see, there was something else." He slid a ring onto her right-hand ring finger—the left had a pearl and emerald ring, held in place by a thick gold band.

Andrew. No. The memories came back and crowded around her, wanting her attention, but she wouldn't think about Andrew now.

The new ring had a setting of greenish gold and a blue translucent stone. Tiny drops of water were snared at its heart. "I found that one in my travels," Moss said, "but I already had a man's ring that belonged to my great-grandfather. You can have this one to keep."

Cynthia fluttered her fingers to see the beads of liquid dance. "I like it so much. May I keep the button?"

"Sure. It was on my school jacket, once upon a time."

She put her arms around his neck and gazed at him. The red tear of a birthmark, almost hidden by his hairline, reminded her of—what? She could hardly think about it now because she was so taken up with the possibility that she had found what she had been hunting.

She remembered the boy standing in the trees, naked, a world away. *The muse.* All at once it seemed that this boy and that one might as well be the same—that each had drawn her into chasing the beautiful. Hadn't the Opal Bone, too, drawn her after him when he planted a seed in the ice? And even Iz-shadow with her glowing needles had called to her and opened a door…

Lowering her arms, she looked over at the morning glory. The thread of a vine seemed to be blossoming inside her, its flowers unfurling in her throat and chest, tendrils winding around her limbs.

"I'd like to stay here forever."

"There's nothing to eat or drink." He reached for her hand and twisted the ring into place on her finger, holding up her hand to admire how it looked.

"But I'm—I'm dead." Her voice rose in surprise at the realization. "Aren't I?"

"You're just dead, as you call it, here—not there—as I'm dead there and not here. But you'll be dead there if you don't go back." Tickled by the absurdity, he laughed. "What I mean is that you'll stop. Go out like a candle. Well, it's a sort of dream logic, I suppose. Maybe I'll just go out like a candle instead. Other places exist," he added. "This is just a minor district. Still, you need to return, or else all sorts of things will be left undone. It's always that way."

"What do you mean?"

He ignored the question, as if it were either obvious or impossible to explain.

She tried again. "Can you come with me?"

"Ah, wouldn't I surprise Teddy!"

"Teddy," she repeated, "Teddy. I wanted to forget him. I tried to replace him with another story. I wonder; maybe that's what I'm doing now. He told me—a lie—about you, I think. He called you a gimp. What's he to do with it?"

Moss shrugged, saying that it didn't matter. "Do I look like a gimp? My legs were always better than his. He pushed me once, and I fell."

Cynthia touched the red droplet of birthmark.

"I can't go," he told her. "Not *here* to *there* to stay. In fragments of places so unexpected that I might have dreamed them, I see it sometimes."

"Teddy," she said, closing her eyes. "He shut the door on me."

"My mother. I'll never forgive him for making her grieve—"

He paused, frowning at the morning glory.

She was still trying to focus on Teddy, though her first thought was gladness that she had found Moss and, more than that, that she had collected, one by one, strange treasures: the path of shining needles; the angel sweeping across the lake in a moving glow; the silvery tree in ice; the minotaur; the green ballroom under the lake.

I am an artist, she thought with wonderment. *That is the thing I am and was made to be.*

And so I came for these images and for these creatures, whether they are glass or flesh or ghost.

I came to follow my changeable, quicksilver muse. To thread the maze. Was following its passageways part of what the Opal Bone had said: to make my myth, to find my story?

She touched the boy's hand, remembering the sound of the door slamming shut. "Did he leave you in the dark? Did he—"

Moss bent over her, and she clung to him, the edges of their bodies overlapping.

"You have to go. But you're a noticing sort of person. I imagine that you'll see me again—maybe just in glimpses. Plenty, even." He tucked a strand of hair behind her ear, his glance going to the needle in her gown. "Like a streak of silver in a golden haystack."

"How?"

He didn't answer, sliding away from her. This time he kept on going, right through the edge of the ballroom and into the outer ice. She called after him that she was lost.

"Lost, found, what's the difference?" But he turned toward her, looking blurry and white-faced at a distance. The glimmering of a memory—the painted form of a boy under the water—floated up.

"Water burial," she said, remembering the flood.

She skated past the flowering Victrola and out the walls of the ballroom.

Perhaps it was "through the ice" that Moss shouted, just before vanishing.

"Oh." The word was a prolonged sigh.

Climbing up the blue stairs from the emerald story, she felt the motes of memory swarming, as if they wanted to join and carry her back home. She thrust them back, her mind only wanting to consider the inhabitants of this world: the boy in the trees, Moss, Iz-shadow, the minotaur, and the angel.

"Guides," she murmured.

Once more she passed Muskrat Castle, now thatched, with frozen flowers blooming on the roof. This time she climbed its ladder and gazed over the lake.

"Moss! Come back to me!" The words rang against the hills. Cynthia felt that he could never be summoned, and though she called, she had no expectation of more than echoes.

In a sunbeam, the angel's tree glittered, bare and silver. Going to it, she found glistening leaves stuck to the surface of Glimmerglass and pods that stood erect on the branches like golden torches. On peering into the ice, she made out a snake knotted around the bole and a ball of fur snuggled below. She sank through, drawing herself onto the other side of the lake by a tangle of silver roots. Far off, she glimpsed a skater in a black cloak, bowed against the wind as he pulled a child's heavily loaded sleigh.

As she walked in the labyrinth by the lake, a needle slipped from her gown, making an infinitesimally small *ping!* as the eye widened to let her in. She glimpsed a path of splinters and droplets of water before threading the eye of the needle and sliding head first into the plush midnight fabric of sleep.

The Silver Tree

The patina was yellow, blue with shadows: her eyes rested on it without any touch of abhorrence for a long time when she woke. Only as she came more fully awake did she know that the thing before her was bone, spilled across a discolored patch of rock. One of the buttons on a school jacket was missing. While the remainder of the clothing had rotted away, the synthetic cloth of the jacket was still mostly intact. The gold and bloodstone ring still circling a finger bone was no doubt the birthday ring. A ledge jutted from a narrow opening in the wall above.

"Pushed."

In the vault of the hill, the word shivered on stone. She wondered at herself, feeling no horror.

Close by, she heard the voices of children. Despite fever, despite weakness, she felt the will to live as the flutter of something akin to triumph. Putting her hand in the pocket of her gown, she found the button safe. An amethyst feather was stuck to the garnet throw. Retrieving a silver needle, she drove it deep into the collar of her robe. On her right-hand ring finger was a transparent blue stone mounted in greenish gold. She would have to labor to remember that these were not simply stray finds, picked up in fever and confusion. She couldn't forget these souvenirs of a stay in darkness, nor that they held meanings and story.

Slowly, with much trembling, she stood and gazed down at the skeleton in the blue school jacket and gray threads that must have once been pants.

"Poor boy."

She moved away, listening for the children's yells. Liquid trickled somewhere close by, and its music of drippage and pause and flow sounded very sweet to Cynthia. When she discovered a runnel of water at the path's edge, she followed until she reached a hillock of rubble and, above it, a narrow opening nearly covered by a loose piece of slate. Ascending the stones, struggling to grab hold of edges where the beams of light poured in: it was not as hard as many other things, though her fingers were bloody before she was done.

172

The lip of the opening where drops had seeped was mossy and soft. She hoisted herself through until her shoulders and arms were free.

A little sprite whirled in the sunshine not twenty yards from the opening, shouting in glee.

"Neddie! Ned!" Her voice sounded like the creaking ghost of a door hinge, but by the third cry he stopped and looked around.

At last he came forward cautiously, taking exaggerated high steps, his arms raised. But when he saw her, thrust partway from the earth, he leaped into the air.

"Ned, it's me."

Coming closer, he squatted before her.

"What're you doing?" He scratched his elbow, picking at a scab. "They're all looking for you. Everybody's here." A gleam of pleasure skimmed over his face. "But I found you!"

"What's the date?"

Cynthia raked the sweaty hair back from her face so she could see him better.

"Friday. It's a Friday." Ned looked as though he would laugh at her. "You know that!"

"I want you to give this to Andrew," she told him, pressing something onto his palm and folding his fingers around it. "Don't drop it."

"Great-uncle Teddy is right there," he said, pointing, "so I'll give it to him." He stood up as if about to race away, and she caught sight of her brother-in-law, whipping a cane through a patch of scrub.

"No! Remember our secret with the key? This is special. It's important not to tell Teddy. He'll just keep it. Give it to Andrew and bring him back—guide him by the hand. Nobody else. Tell him you were the clever one who discovered me and that you need to take him here." Her whisper sounded no stronger than two burnished leaves of silver, rubbed lightly together.

Ned squatted again, inspecting her. "What happened to you?"

"Lots. Right now, what's in your hand is our secret, okay? Andrew. By the hand. Hurry."

"I hear a crackly sound."

"It's my breath, Neddie—I've been sick. Go on. Please?"

Her knees felt crushed against the debris, and she wasn't sure how long she could remain there, jammed between rocks and light.

"Neddie! What are you doing?" Lizzie's voice wafted over from the trees.

The little boy didn't answer but stared at Cynthia's bloody fingernails for a moment, as if puzzled, before bolting down the slope. But Teddy looked about, and when he caught sight of her, he stopped thrashing the weeds, his cane in the air. Certain that she could not retreat and climb the heap of stones again, she seized hold of a clump of grass—but what if he struck at her and forced her inside the cave and sealed the gap? Who would believe little Ned, even with what he held in his hand? His story would all be put down to a little boy's fancies.

She could hear the boy calling for his grandfather and then screaming for him, louder and louder. Her brother-in-law hurried across the slope, bending to pry up and grasp a cobble. Though she had painted him, Cynthia had forgotten how powerful his upper arms were. He rocked slightly as he ran, and she realized that he, not Moss, had been the one with the limp.

"No," he choked out, lifting the weapon.

"Drew! Help me!" Lizzie shouted to her brother as she caught sight of the pale hair and face rising from the earth.

Teddy reeled to face his great-niece.

"Yes. Help me," he repeated. The voice was hoarse. "We can use this stone to make the hole larger." Dropping onto his knees, he let it roll from his hand.

He watched, crouched like an animal in the scrub, as the brother and sister hauled her from the mossy gap in the hill and into the light.

"Lizzie," Cynthia whispered, "don't you leave me."

Far more panicked by what he saw than Neddie had been, Drew raced off, shrieking for his grandfather. Lizzie cradled her step-grandmother's bleeding hand as Teddy groaned, pushing himself onto his feet with the cane, and started unsteadily down the slope.

Parched and aching, still feverish, Cynthia lay on the moss and stared up at the crown of trees on the hilltop. She felt as strange as a butterfly unfolding after the dark, cramped dream of a chrysalis. Her body burned with what seemed transfiguration as the glory of sun seared her. It dazzled her eyes with a glare like snow-covered Glimmerglass on a sunny day. Momentarily she glimpsed a figure crossing an opening in the grove, though perhaps it was only a mote swirling across the light.

Just then she cried out, feeling a flood of newness and freedom. She had opened up like a Chinese parasol in the hand of an angel. Colors were fresh and saturated in her sight, and she had the sudden sweeping sense of magic rising like sap through the outer world.

Dimly she recalled the days before she had entered the hill—the rumors of war, the shadows looming, and the voices of Babel. Birds had fallen from the sky. A dying soldier had bled from his mouth as a chaplain recited the 23rd Psalm. A terrorist had killed a poet, and children in their Sunday clothes had died.

The world might be the same, but she was not.

In her mind was a silver tree hung with images. She felt more than knew what they meant and what their stories were. *Our Lady of the Needles. A seed, a tree upside down in ice. The angel slicing through Glimmerglass, Muskrat Castle, the lake and hills, and the almost-visible demons seething in the air close by. Moss, awakening her from slumber. The morning glory ballroom. The beautiful patina of the bones. Her body caught in the mossy gap, thrust into sunshine.*

There were bounds to this life and only so much time until her heart and mind ceased—until she was planted like a seed that waits without waiting in the dark ground. But there were hours left to transmute these things into pictures. She had, though late, found her way.

Moss.

What was he?

As she lay in the almost unbearable brilliance, it seemed to her that he was, after all, twin to the figure she had glimpsed in the trees and painted so long ago, a boy venturing naked and heartbroken into the old world he had left behind. They had led her on, her guides and muses, into strange regions. Had she dreamed Moss and the others—called them to her out of need and longing? Oh, she was forgetting them! But surely she would remember the picture of Moss lending her ballast, or waltzing—inside an emerald—with a hand at her waist. Surely she could embody that lyric moment when their two figures merged into one angelic flesh, branched with veins of light.

Flesh of my flesh.

The day's brightness seemed to pour through her skin until she was a Chinese lantern, filled with intense light and heat. She caught a glimpse of Lizzie, peering into her face. The girl clutched at her fingers, as if to make sure this newfound grandmother would not get away from her. The others were louder now, rushing toward her.

Cynthia stared into the sun, the tears sliding through grime into her knotted hair, until she heard Andrew's voice and let go and fell like a star into the darkness of sleep.

Philip

On Sunday, she finally woke up in a white hospital room, with long gauzy curtains blowing across the floor. No longer feverish, she felt as though a stone had been lifted from her chest, lending her new strength, though the mirror opposite showed cuts on face and arms. Bruise marks indicated where IV lines must have been.

Her husband was standing at the door with a young man, half familiar. When Andrew saw that Cynthia had awakened, he came in and seized her hands and kissed her on the forehead.

"I flew home when I finally got hold of Teddy, and he told me that you'd been gone for days. I couldn't reach either one of you and didn't know what had happened, but thank God, you're all right. You were so dehydrated, you might have died in the hill. And pneumonia—no wonder you slept so long. I can't understand why he thought you might've gone away without a word. Maybe because you'd parked your car above the old gardener's cottage, since Teddy says he didn't know it was there. Or maybe he's going a bit dotty."

"It doesn't matter now," Cynthia said, "not to us."

When the young man leaned in the doorway to tell Andrew that he would meet him in the lobby later on, they both called for him to come in.

"My youngest nephew—our nephew Philip—visiting from out of town," Andrew announced. "When something goes wrong, the Wilds turn out in force."

"That's right," the boy said, a little shyly. "I'm sorry to meet you like this—it would have been better another way."

But Cynthia was staring at his irregular but handsome features.

"Doesn't Philip look so very much like Moss," she exclaimed. As is often the way with someone who has suffered and been ill, easy tears sprang to her eyes. "He could be Moss, almost, if only he had a little drop like blood on his forehead."

Much of the journey in the hill had grown obscure to her, but she had not yet lost his face—joyful, as if peering out from a dream. What remained indelible was a series of images.

Andrew looked at her strangely and plucked something from his pocket, turning it over between his fingers. She held out a hand and accepted the button with its image of two griffins.

"Yes, I found him there." Her voice was still low, wounded and weak. "I'm pretty sure that I can find the way to the bones. Once I'm home, we'll have to bring what's left of him away. Though he'll always be lingering there, in some fashion, I suppose."

They sat in silence for a while, the others not quite knowing what to say in response, until Philip mentioned the masses of white flowers that were mounded in a corner. They were in keeping with Cynthia's pallor and the starkness of the room.

The two men had to bend to hear her words: "Lovely petals. Like flesh of angels."

When a nurse came on quiet feet to remind them that the patient should not be allowed to grow tired, Cynthia caught hold of Philip's hand and then let go.

"Before you leave town, I'd like to sketch you," she said, "and take some photographs. I want to paint Moss, more than anything, when I get back to Sea House. I want to make my lost painting over again. And there are others in my mind. You could be my model. Even your eyes are like his, blue with streaks of green—"

Andrew kissed her on the mouth. "Would you like to see Teddy? I think he was an awful fool not to realize and let me know that something was the matter, but he'd like to see you."

When she closed her eyes, Cynthia's face looked like a mask of alabaster, pale and still.

"He has the key," she murmured. "When you go home, you must take it from him. Promise me."

The shadow from Andrew's body passed over her eyes, and she opened them again.

"Cynthia, I don't understand," he said slowly, looking down at her.

"Don't worry. It's just that," she said, "he took it from the floor or out of the lock—something. But you must go and put it somewhere safe for me, so we don't lose it again."

He nodded. "As soon as I reach home, I will speak to Teddy and get the key. I promise you."

"Good." She stared up at him without speaking, more tired than she had felt since emerging from the cave.

She closed her eyes again, and sensed that Andrew was waiting to see if there was more. He crouched beside the bed, sliding his hand under hers. Cynthia's fingers stirred faintly against his palm.

"And yes, I would like very much to see him," she said at last. "Perhaps you would be so good as to bring my sweet little Ned at the same time. I have a wish to see them together."

The Banishing

In the evening, Teddy and Ned came for a visit. The window by Cynthia's hospital bed had darkened to twilight. A small pot of violets of the same dusky blue, swaddled in green foil, now relieved the whiteness of the room.

"I found you," Ned said with satisfaction, running inside and climbing onto the bed close beside her. Cynthia put her arms around him and laid her cheek against his hair.

"You look…very well. Considering." Teddy paused in the door, holding the offering of a plant. The blades were at stiff attention above the clay pot with its dramatic shroud of blood-colored foil and slash of black ribbon. He looked slantwise at her, seeming to judge her reaction.

"I am well or will be soon enough," she said, snuggling Ned close. "The Wrens were just here, and we had a good visit. I'll be going home tomorrow morning."

"Such a strange thing. I thought there was no key to the hill. I'm so glad you are safe." He let out a sigh and came closer to the bed and held out his hand.

She didn't respond.

"Will you give me your hand?"

"Another, more public time," she said, "when I must. I should've been wary. Didn't Lydia see something wrong in your portrait? My hands saw it, my eye—but still I didn't know. Now I know."

"What on earth do you mean?" He laughed and set the sansevieria on a table.

"I mean Moss, pushed from a ledge, and I mean his mother who killed herself for grief. And I even mean the sound of a closing door at my back." Her fingers strayed to the child's silky hair. "Neddie, did you know that your great-uncle is moving into the gatehouse? That's where he's going to live from now on."

Teddy started, and the boy stopped fooling with an amethyst feather that he had picked up from the nightstand and looked at her.

"Why?"

183

"Oh, that's his business, I suppose. But all the same, he will go there and not live at Sea House anymore, ever again."

Teddy had taken out a large handkerchief and mopped at his forehead. His hand was trembling.

The boy took no notice, curling against Cynthia. He put one arm around her waist and, with the other, twirled the feather between his fingers.

"What do you think you're playing at? No one has ever accused me of any ill action—nothing has been proven against me—you're clearly sick. They told us not to tire you." After a moment of calm, he burst out again: "I belong at Sea House more than you do. Or ever will."

She gave him a stare as blue as Glimmerglass on a late autumn day.

"Oh, I belong there more than you can imagine. And Moss belongs at Sea House too. We talked in the hill, and I know quite enough about you, Teddy once called *Theo*. It's no wonder to me that Moss Wild bore a blood-red tear on his face when he was born."

"You're delirious, I believe." Teddy fumbled at his vest.

It was, Cynthia noted, the Lincoln green one with a pattern of keys. A button was stitched in place with thread that, to her eyes, was slightly wrong in color. It reminded her of Moss and another lost and found button.

"I have never been better. Never," she repeated. "You would be surprised at how very well I am. And at how much I know."

184

"You are—what do want from me?" He jerked at the handkerchief, forcing it into a waistcoat pocket. "Would you shove me into the dark and lock the door? What kind of unfairness is in your mind?"

"I know what you did long ago in the maze. I saw the place where Moss fell." Cynthia drew the feather from Neddie's fingers and tickled his nose with it. She considered its beauty, holding the vane upright.

"But," she said, "I won't revenge myself on you. You have made a sort of monster of me, but not that kind, not your kind. And so I have the right to make my demands. You see, I'm not afraid of you or the hill—I don't believe I'm afraid of anything now."

She looked at him, hunched in his jacket against the backdrop of white flowers. He looked a comic figure with his red nose and his belly snug under a waistcoat. But he was not.

"Because I am a master of the labyrinth." The peculiar, confident claim surprised her; she hadn't realized what she would say. *Was it true?* "I can come and go as I please. Because I have allied myself to something—what exactly it is doesn't matter to you—beyond this daily world. That is the kind of monster I am."

He appeared diminished and put his hands in his jacket pockets with the air of a man seeking to hide them.

"Isn't the gatehouse empty?" She was quite sure it was so.

"Yes."

"You must go there, Teddy. That is my wish. You will be one lone dwarf of a man in the seven dwarves' cottage,

185

with the pomegranates on the ceiling and the dragonish salamanders in the cellar. It is not your death in the maze. It is not jail. I have no idea what will emerge when the bones of your cousin are collected from the dark—from our strange little otherworld in the hill. I don't try to prove because I cannot, but I know. And you—we are so close now because we both know some of the same secrets about how I was locked in the maze. And about Moss and how he vanished."

She paused, one hand raised to stop him from speaking.

"You must never live at Sea House again. That's my second wish. And not one flicker of unwillingness will you show to your half-brother. Nor will you attempt to divide us in any way. My third: you must never try to hurt me or mine. If you do, there will be consequences because I intend to prepare documents, just in case. And here is one more. I want you to confess your secrets to Hale Wren and would like to know that you have done so."

Teddy gazed at her, and only the twitch of a muscle near one eye showed that he was discomposed.

"This is a kind of madness, Cynthia. You can't make me do these things—you know nothing against me."

She laughed playfully, softly, as if teasing him. "To you, it seems so unfair. Doesn't it? You've known Andrew much longer than I have. Old family in Cooper Patent outweighs a world of strangers. Half a brother must count more than a stranger allied by mere marriage—by a handful of words that can be broken. But you've not known him

186

every way I have. I'm already closer than you could ever be."

Teddy didn't answer. He had moved toward the dark rectangle of the open door that now threatened to swallow him.

"You were talking about worlds." Neddie frowned at her.

"Maybe I was just showing off a little. Carried away." Cynthia squeezed him. "You weren't listening to any of that, were you? I thought you were drifting off to the Land of Nod. It's late."

"And what were you saying about monsters?" Ned reached for the feather.

"Nothing, sweetheart. Not monsters with horns and beaks and human faces on the backs of fish, or whatever it is that scares you. Just the ways that people act like monsters or become strange sometimes. I felt very odd when I was lost. But I'll be going home tomorrow, and soon you and I can go dig for fossils and see what we find. All right?"

He nodded, drawing the feather along her arm.

"Now please don't take my feather. I need it—I'm going to use it in a painting. I might even paint with it," she told him. "It looks good and strong and might make an especially good brush."

"Where did you get it?"

"I'm not entirely sure, but my memory says that I got it from an angel."

"Really?" He handed over the feather with a moue of regret and afterward began fingering the controls of the hospital bed, pretending to call the night nurse.

187

Cynthia looked across at her brother-in-law.

"Listen," she said. "You ought to confess to Hale Wren. Then tell me in his hearing that you have confessed to a mortal sin, having to do with the fall of man. The fall of a particular young man, that is. I do not know what might or might not be proven by some able forensic work, looking at certain fine, broken threads wrapped around a skeleton's finger bones. But I do know that you are harboring darkness and need to find some light."

"I see that you want to entrap me into telling falsehoods for your satisfaction." His voice was shrill, but when he met her eyes, he looked away. "But I will go," he added, "since that is your pleasure." He spoke the word *pleasure* as though it were a foul-tasting lozenge in his mouth.

"I wouldn't lie if I were you, Theodore Wild. Go on. And take your snake plant with you. Consider it a house-warming gift from me and your darling cousin Moss. And now let me be alone with this dear little boy." Cynthia leaned back against the pillows and closed her eyes. When she opened them again, the garden gnome had vanished.

Ned patted her head. "Was he angry?"

"Not at you, Neddie. He knew it was time to go. He just wasn't so happy about it as he might have been."

In a few minutes, Andrew appeared at the door and stood watching Ned comb his fingers through Cynthia's hair.

"I really wanted that feather," the boy said dreamily.

188

"You remind me later on. Maybe I'll give it to you someday, when you're a young man and can look after it properly."

"Yes!" He inspected the cuts on her face and gave her a kiss before running to his grandfather.

"Great-uncle Teddy is moving, did you know?" He took Andrew's hand and swung it to get his attention. "He said so."

Mistress of Worlds

The sheets were soft and clean and smelled pleasantly of lavender. Cynthia was home again, spooned against her husband's side. The key lay in a silk drawstring bag under her pillow.

She had arrived in time for lunch and found that Teddy was already gone, ensconced in the gatehouse. The young cousins from out of town had moved him in the roughshod, slapdash way of teenagers, tossing furniture about and dumping treasures unceremoniously into paper bags and boxes.

In the afternoon, she sat in the garden and sketched the unfamiliar relatives and made some studies of Philip's face and hands. Andrew brought a light blanket to tuck around her after she fell asleep with a pencil between her fingers. The parasol he had brought from Chinatown shaded her face. Although she had insisted that Iz be invited, Cynthia dozed through the visit, waking only when her finger was pricked by the needle in her pocket. She was disappointed, having resolved to start getting to know Iz, and she had intended to ask about the little statue of Somnium, the minotaur.

"We ought to ask her more often," she said, head on Andrew's shoulder. "I understand Iz better now. Besides, I want to do a painting or two of her."

"That's a bit mercenary-sounding." He drew back to look her in the face.

"The trouble with artists, isn't it?"

She felt closer to Andrew in some ways, more grateful for his affection and sympathy, though it felt as though she had been away from him for a very long time. He didn't ask about the breach with Teddy, but he had gone quiet when the cousins returned from the gatehouse, high-spirited and ravenous. Cynthia would have to work to regain what she and Andrew had been before, though that was all right and worth the doing.

Like a stay in a fairy mound, her time in the hill had tugged at and rearranged the world. It was a loss, but a greater gain. With its two drops that trembled like meltwater trapped in hollows of frozen Glimmerglass, the ring made a counterbalance to the pearl and emerald ring and

191

the gold band that her husband had placed on her finger, and expressed a hidden allegiance that she had not yet fully divined.

Trust what happened, she thought, *no matter how it came and went. No matter what it was. No matter how these treasures — the ring and button from Moss, the feather from Bone, the needle from Iz-shadow — were won.*

The worlds were folded together like origami, and how they were joined was a mystery. Even in this realm, her secluded life on the edge of Glimmerglass led to a larger one of grief and pain, the wild world beyond the wild wood. She supposed, in the end, that the two worlds ought not to be separated. How tired she was, grateful that night had come at last so that she could curl in the darkness beside Andrew without speaking. Soon she would return to the hill and help recover the bones; the search party was even now being arranged, though they would wait another week until she grew stronger.

Sometimes she doubted that the murder could ever be proven, but she never faltered in her belief that the death was no accident. And pursuing her own case would have meant her word against Teddy's, and deep division in Andrew's mind. No, she would not attempt to convict Teddy further than she had already done by ousting him from Sea House. The bones would convict him if they could.

The clock struck 2:00 a.m.

She slipped out of bed and walked through the darkened house. The last of the visiting cousins had gone to bed, and the sheets pulled from furniture in seldom-used rooms lay in drifts outside the doors. It was good to have the house occupied by more than two people. Moonlight showed her the black silhouette faces of Wild husbands and wives and children from long ago as she passed by.

A silver key sparkled like a star caged between her fingers.

The door yawned onto the dark.

As ever, the hill spoke its one long word of susurrus. Cynthia listened to the sound as to the pure waves of creation. There was no stop, no start to its utterance. The syllables sang, as green as the sea and as mysterious as Glimmerglass and all the little streams that raced pell-mell toward its heart, flooding and dripping and bearing away the beautiful drowned figure of the boy in her painting. When Cynthia closed her eyes, his white face looked out from the emerald tide.

Word without end, amen.

The phrase streamed through her hearing and was gone, without her being entirely aware whether she had spoken, or dreamed, or caught the sound of another's voice.

She felt drawn—didn't she, though!—but closed and locked the door.

Born during illness and pain, her bright, scattered memories now made no more of a coherent narrative than the colors thrown from a stained-glass window onto the church pavement, their story lost. But they were no less compelling for being shards of something larger.

So many things were a twisted journey, with surprises at the heart. She had been changed into a kind of spy,

Cynthia reflected, because what she wanted was to infiltrate this realm with the other: to put it all on canvas.

"To seed the ice. To walk both sides—all sides—of Glimmerglass."

These half-understood words, whispered in the night, thrilled her. She closed her eyes once more, seeking a deeper darkness. Was the key a seed? It burned in the blackness like a star in a tomb. The word inside the hill went on forever, and the silver tree with its blossoms and leaves that meant paintings to come shot up in her mind like an everlasting fountain.